first edition

Published with the generous assistance of the Canada Council for the Arts and the Ontario Arts Council. Coach House Books also acknowledges the support of the Government of Canada through the Canada Book Fund and the Government of Ontario through the Ontario Book Publishing Tax Credit.

CANADIAN CATALOGUING IN PUBLICATION DATA

Farrell, Dan, 1963-
The inkblot record

Poems.
ISBN 1-55245-053-8

I. Title.

PS8561.A77I54 2000 C811'.54 C00-931536-5
PR9199.3.F358I54 2000

The Inkblot Record

The Inkblot Record

Dan Farrell

Coach House Books

A bagpipe. A bat. A bat. A bat. A bat or a butterfly I guess, do I have to tell which? A bear. A beaver, another beaver. A bell. A bell. A big bat. A big bat with antennas. A big giant fly. A big man. A bird. A blood splotch. A blue mist in middle with dim forms in it. A buffalo hide. A butterfly. A butterfly. A butterfly. A butterfly. A butterfly being torn apart. A butterfly house 'cause that looks like a butterfly. A butterfly, I know how to make these too. A butterfly, see the wings and feet? A butterfly with thorns. A carving of an animal climbing on side of mountain. A castle – like in a movie – that's hidden away. A cat reaching out. A caterpillar. A child's socks, just the color and shape. A Christmas tree. A clam. A closed mouth, a cupid's bow. A cloud. A cloud is not formed any specific way. A couple of kids playing Indian having a good time. A couple of spiders pushing them closer together. A couple of – what is it that has tentacles? A dance movement. A dead cat falling down. A dead turtle with lots of heads, shell may be folded over – no. A deer's head. A devil's mask. A dog looking for a favor, a biscuit. A dog sitting on his haunches waiting for a command. A dog wouldn't be upright. A dog's face. A dragonfly buzzing around. A face. A face mask. A face mask a samurai would wear. A fantastic shimmering scene. A few eggs dropped around here and some splashed here. A flower opening out, budding. A foot. A formal garden in spring with an iron fence at the end, two banks of pink azaleas. A fountain spray, like water shooting. A fraternity paddle. A giant. A giant with tre-mendous feet coming at me. A gunshot wound, with blood dripping out of it. A hammered piece of metal, the bumpy effect. A hand in symbolic prayer. A hand-carved statue inside some container. A heart. A hide, jagged pointed edges, tail on pole, rest hanging down spread out.

A hide spread out. A highway under construction. A hole in the ground, maybe like a well. A hole through the wall. A jackknife dive into the sea. A leafy tree. A leg, could be an animal walking toward you. A leg of some kind of meat. A long one. A lot of organs vaguely connected with bits of bone and nerve in the middle. A lot of times you don't know what to expect. A magic candle sends off different colors of light. A man I met. A man leaning back balancing something, a juggler act. A man sitting on a tree stump. A man with a cigarette in his mouth. A map of America. A maple seed in here. A mist. A mist, probably a fine morning mist like you see in the country, it may be clearing. A modernistic painting. A mole. A mole in climbing position but not moving. A nuclear reactor exploding, now this is a hard one, just a nuclear reactor exploding, I've seen pictures of one, but no one's ever seen it like this. A pair of gloves. A pawnbroker's balls. A pelt, caught and split down the center and stretched to dry. A penis. A person. A person with two heads in between. A photograph, a negative that has been ruined out of focus. A photographic map like we used to get in the army. A piece of moldy bread. A pig romping. A polar bear, must be climbing up a sheer cliff, he must have glue on his feet. A pole, with rats standing up. A portrait. A potato chip. A problem in painting. A pussycat, the whole thing. A rainbow mix-up. A red mark on its nose. A rocket. A rocket shooting off its runway. A rough furriness, animal-like. A secret map, like the CIA has all the time. A single woman, buttocks. A soft, fluffy, stuffed bunny. A spaceship. A spinal tap, my brother had one years ago, he was in a new part of the hospital, he was frightened and lonely, he wanted me to visit him, but I didn't feel I was enough support to him. A spinning mechanism. A stingray, kind of fish. A storm cloud, because of its fullness. A summer cottage we used to go to, the atmosphere of the cottage bothered me. A sunrise. A topographical map. A toy animal. A tree. A tuning fork, it has the big handle and the narrow vibrator part. A valley. A variety of fish belonging to shark family with sucker in front. A very hard climb up, a difficult mountain to climb. A very square butterfly being torn apart. A Viking ship with headmast. A volcano exploding. A war statue of two soldiers in hand-to-hand combat. A wishbone in the center. A woman diving. A woman with head cut off and two gentlemen at her side that look like ghosts. A woman with two heads reaching out for help. About half of the ship is here. Actively enclosing and protecting quality about the top. After a storm, all puffed up and you can crack them, not the exact color, but it's light and cool-looking. Again, the sex symbol. Again, the sex thing on the bottom. Aha, better, I like colors, maybe it's a tree up here, a magic tree. *Alice in Wonderland* animals climbing rocks. Alimentary canal, double heart, a big spinal column and feces. Alive, it seems to be resisting the fall. All creatures need covering and defenses to protect themselves. All have some relief map look. All look like plains – like one of those maps – areas to represent different types of land, cultivated or high hilly areas. All of it looks like a mask, cat face. All of this looks like a dead, burnt-up stump of an old tree and here at the top is an old owl, the wise old owl, all crouched into a ball so you can only see the head and he's staring right out at you, see the round body, up here, see it? All of this white part, it just has the same shape as a mushroom. All rest part of mountains. All sitting or standing on branches somewhere. All the blood around so it must be one. All the red is the veins with the blood coming out and this one is the heart, and the rest of it is the body. All the stuff, the colors, are running together like it was melting in the sun. All these seem to have – looks like a uterus. All those colors, that's like paint. All you can see is her hair, which would be blonde or white, and her face, which is darker, is the white part so you can't tell who she is, she has a French-style hairdo with the puff on top and little wisps coming out at the sides. Almost a dance movement. Almost in an eagle costume, with wings, standing on top of a craggy hill. Almost looks like a centipede, projecting legs. Almost looks like a typical wizard casting a spell, imaginary wand. Also a man trying to fly, a flying machine on his back, but it isn't working very well, he's pretty stupid, he could work on more important things than trying to fly. Also looks like a red bow tie, makes me think of my father's wild ties, that's something I like about him. Also looks like roosters – or chickens or fowl – I don't know much about that. Also looks like the lower half of a bowlegged cowboy, you don't see the upper half but just the trunk and the spread-apart legs, it's ridiculous. Also – these ladies look like French dancing ladies. Always just so into herself, partly because she just drank so much, into another world, gave herself, in some ways took care of us, but didn't give emotionally, didn't care about us. Am I really supposed to tell you what this looks like to me? Amorphous like a fungus, they are almost colorless. An abstract painting of some kind. An anal cavity. An anal thermometer. An anatomical drawing, center of bony structure, visceral areas demarcated in color, lungs, stomach and lower organs. An animal head, some kind of terrier. An animal jumping, I don't know why, maybe he's scared like me, and he is seeing himself down here in the water. An animal pelt.

An eel. An erect penis. An existential crab. An explosive center, forms floating around the calm after the storm. An hourglass. An hourglass – not a good one – distorts time because not same size on top and bottom. An ornamental statue, Indian in nature, sort of a totem pole. An underwater sea scene. An unreal carnival-like Halloween party, shoes like cloven hoofs, bodies bent. An x-ray of alimentary canal, double heart, spinal column and feces. An x-ray of somebody's spinal cord. And a butterfly, I got a lot outta this one. And a cat. And a flower. And a frog's face. And a king's court. And a nuclear bomb exploding. And a pair of shears, clip clip. And a penis being circumcised, that's it. And all the pieces look like they've been breaded, probably with cracker meal, or some are. And an ant face. And here it's black and this is white. And it's a rain cloud, all the different dark colors make it like a rain cloud. And it's a raven. And rockets. And the abominable snowman, ha ha ha, he's like, weird, like they built him funny or maybe he's built so his feet are out forward, more like this and his little head is back more. And the clumsy feet. And the tendrils on the wing, that's like a moth, but wings are not shaped like a moth and the body's like a bat's. And these little streamers and stuff. And this is like a lap dog sitting at the woman's feet, his head is on a level with her hand, she is feeding him. And this part does not belong. And two bears trying to climb a tree. And two jellyfish. And up here there's two more eating this stick. Angry and ghoulish type with the dark eyes. Angular faces, angling back, give the sense of pulling away instead of helping, tugging or trying to gain control. Animal figure. Animal figure made of white, hooded effect almost to eyes. Animals. Animals. Animal's feet and legs, half of an animal standing up that way.

Animal's head. Another flower maybe, like a tulip, like they plant in the parks. Another one! Antenna of insect here. Antennae of insect. Antlers. Ants taking little pieces of food. Any pictures I've seen of 'em have these two little tails and head and these wings, so evenly apart like this. Apron tied up behind her. Are these really supposed to be something? Are you writing down everything I say? Arm bent, body in motion, female leg. Arm bent, body reclining, female leg. Armadillos, one on each side with just the legs sticking out, the rest is all in the shell. Arms behind backs, each have an identical white circle on chest. Arms behind their backs. Arms come down, disappear because picture's not complete, maybe they're under the blanket. Arms droop off, lungs in middle, can't see the ribs, that shows person has bad case of TB. Arms not long enough to come out of the costume because it's really two people, one sitting on top of the other. Arms turned out, towards sides (*demonstrates*). As if the wings made them look as though they should be feared. At a sixty-degree angle, form an equilibrium triangle. At first, the older figure, he was an older version of this one. Babies or dwarfs, anyway pink. Baby's booties. Baby's pink buttocks. Back of rabbit's ears. Back of skull. Back of the head of a rabbit, that's all. Back toward us, standing up. Badly dried and cut because of the dark and light spots in here. Bald, grotesque, gleeful clowns, like tall hats, faces sticking out, playful. Balloon, shiny, round object. Balls of cotton. Barefooted, legs and hips, head seems divided in two parts, hands in mittens, see legs through dress, transparent dress. Basin in a mountain. Bat. Bat. Bat in flight, wings spread out, attached to body. Bat with rodent-like ears. Beak of a bird. Bear. Bears going sideways on coat of arms. Bears sitting on their hind legs facing in opposite directions.

Beautiful green ball dress. Beautiful, it's nothing, just a reflection, at least three miles away, see evergreen trees and looks like smoke aurora around fire, heavy black smoke, forest back here. Beautiful reflection, very far away. Because eyes drawn down. Because he used to go out of control when I was young, out of anger. Because here's its head, body, arms on the sides, big feet, with something sticking up in the middle; that's why I call it a monster with a pogo stick. Because here's the back (*imitates sitting*), yeah, they're shaped round. Because here's the wings and here's the hole part. Because here's their legs, and there's where their legs are connected to their bodies, goes up to their chest, their head. Because I couldn't see the head I assumed a soft substance. Because it goes out like this (*traces outline with finger*). Because it has so many colors. Because it has the green smoke coming out of it, and anything that takes off must have smoke coming out of it. Because it has the shape of the wings, the antennas and the little feet. Because it has these fur things sticking out and the whiskers. Because it looks like a big clown here and it's just going up. Because it's a triangle. Because it's black, it has a shape kind of like a point, so it looks like a bird with wings, and it has a hole cut in it. Because its feet are up, they're not on the grass. Because it's got this. Because it's got wings and the ears are up and it's flying. Because it's gray and rectangle. Because it's green and looks like weeds. Because it's green, with the trunk, straight down the middle, here. Because it's kind of splattered out and black. Because it's kinda big and it's kinda legs here. Because it's kinda like this (*pantomimes stomping*). Because it's kinda shaped like one. Because it's kinda up like this (*traces tail with finger*). Because it's like this. Because it's on a rock.

Because it's round. Because it's shaped like cotton candy and it has the stick. Because it's shaped like one and it's kinda big and it's stomping. Because it's splattered out. Because it's stomping around. Because it's straight and long and has these things to step on. Because it's too rigid, not a beautiful butterfly, supposed to be smooth and round. Because its wings are moving. Because just has such a big foot – feet I mean – and such a little head, that it looks funny I guess. Because of the costume, eagle dance (*demonstrates*). Because of the line of bones. Because of the shape. Because of the shape of these humps, which are their heads. Because of the tuft of hair on the bottom that's like the tuft on a cat's chin. Because of the two protrusions on top. Because of the way it's shaped. Because old ladies had to be in a rocking chair, but these handles, going back perpendicular rather than curving back. Because see the shapes, prints, see, you know, like ink prints. Because somebody jumped in it. Because such – so wide (*traces with finger*). Because the way they are dressed. Because these are their ugly teeth and pointed hats. Because they have a little bit of dark skin and the feathers. Because they have their paws on the thing, like this (*imitates with her own body*). Because they're exhausted, spent all their lives eating people up. Because they're kinda long and kinda long here and here. Because they're kinda shaped like 'em. Because they're long. Because they're rectangle. Because this ear is kinda large and it looks like it's standing on a rock and it's got a tail. Because this is their – kinda like (*points to herself sitting*), it's like this part (*points to her lower torso and upper legs*). Because this part is kinda splattered up. Beetles are so busy arguing with one another, they don't see something bigger coming at them. Beets, red; cabbages, green;

carrots, orange. Before, the Turks also looked like women. Beginning of armorial or escutcheon plate. Being afraid. Being slapped or being hugged. Below the elephants it sort of looks like they're standing on a red butterfly or moth. Belted with bustle, bust, an incomplete manikin. Bending over with hands on the head of an ant or insect, it's got jaws and teeth. Big angry waves with foam on top, large waves ready to splash. Big furry monster. Big pieces of stone worn down by water. Birds. Birds perched, wings out, up. Black hair strewn all over barber's floor. Black Sabbath. Black smoke smudges. Blackness and shape of insignia make me think of airman's death. Blah, that's an ugly thing, like some sort of creature, like a big monster with big feet and a small head, it must be dumb because the head is so small. Blood. Blood. Blood dripping down. Blowing, anyway, or breathing, could be either. Blue eyes. Blue faces, blowing into some kind of apparatus. Blue flags on a twin standard. Blue, my favorite color, looks soft, satiny and luxurious. Blue sky. Blurred man. Body, arms, hands, red boots and red turbans, eyes. Body not actually constructed that way – color – very often in anatomy books. Bomber would be without a fuselage. Boots or overshoes, just the shape. Boots, skirt is tight-waisted, breast, neck, great Russian fur hats, texture of gray white fur. Both are dead to me. Both have arms extended. Bottom looks like a little house. Bottom part looks like that same sex symbol again – Jesus. Bottom red and top orange, mostly in orange are flames. Bow tie in middle symbolic of party color. Boy, I'm beat, this is a hard test, I hope you don't have to do it every day. Breasts, hips, hands up, skirts cover their feet, no heads. Brontë sisters, *Wuthering Heights* and *Jane Eyre*. Brown spaniels; English spaniels with floppy ears. Brownish color of head of Airedale.

Bug's face magnified. Bulls. Bunny with peculiar side-whiskers, two ears, heavy eyes, shape of head. Burdened, a Carmen Miranda sort of thing, velvety fluff, arms out. Bushy and full, looks like foliage. But also reminds me of feelings I have towards my father and someone I went out with, similar to my father. But ghosts I'm not afraid of, it's the spiders and rats (*laughs*). But guys get in and loot the temple, steal the diamond eyes. But it doesn't count. But it doesn't look like anything. But no bottom of a body, just head and front legs, looking behind from where it's hanging from. But the antennae are off. But the bottom color resembles sherbet. But this one looks like it has feet or legs, cut out here and here, so I thought of a bearskin. Butterflies. Butterfly. Butterfly in center, wings and body. Butterfly, right in middle. Butterfly, shape only, the body here. Cacti. Camel that would be used in fighting. Can I look the other way too, like this (*inverts card*)? Can I turn it over? Can see legs over the other's shoulders. Can see the tightly curled center, the outer portion slowly opening, unfurling, looks like these slow motion films they make of plant action. Can you turn these things? Cancan dances, head back, arms, legs, skirt. Cancan girls. Cannibals have something to do with it, maybe heat from the pot. Can't do much on that one either. Can't see expressions, only eyes can be seen, like a motorcycle helmet. Can't see parts in relation to one another; figured it out in terms of the contrast: wings, small body, two antennae. Canyon, green plants, waterfall and foam through here, not much life in it, just steady. Caps, noses, scrawny incomplete figures, standing there. Caricature of men bowing to center figure. Carrot. Cat head and whiskers. Caterpillar-type feet here point inward, sort of like standing up, apparatus leaning against chest.

Caterpillars, the dark sides, the tree in the center and the side extensions are tree branches. Cat-like head with whiskers. Cat's whiskers but no cat, just whiskers. 'Cause all the colors mix up together. 'Cause it has different colors. 'Cause it has eyes like an alligator. 'Cause it – I just think that this is the cat, I just think it looks like a cat. 'Cause it just is the shape of one. 'Cause it looks like a butterfly right there. 'Cause it looks like it, different things. 'Cause it looks like it was real gooey. 'Cause it looks like it's a bat, bat's feet. 'Cause it's brown? 'Cause it's got these two things right here and it looks like a bee. 'Cause it's kinda big. 'Cause it's orange. 'Cause it's red. 'Cause it's shaped like a fly and looks like a fly. 'Cause of the different colors. 'Cause of the wing going out, shaped like an angel. 'Cause they are yellow. 'Cause they're big. 'Cause they're little. 'Cause they're sorta little. 'Cause, they're standing so they remain as far apart as possible. 'Cause they're yellow and they're little. 'Cause this looks like birds. Caution, uncertainty. Center again, lower part triangular in shape. Center organ, line of opening, dark area around, black hair around the opening. Central part looks like some sort of urn or a vase or something like that. Central portion looks like stunted tree been cut off. Chagall. Chalky pastel colors. Chiffon handkerchief here, gowned and gloved in same color. Child sticking its tongue out. Children being ostracized by their parents. Chinese hands with long fingers coming down. Chinese lanterns let down from strings, shape and color. Christmas colors. Church. Claws, something to grab something with. Climbing up rocks. Clothesline with clothes hanging on it. Cloud-like effect here. Clowns playing pattycake, hands come together. Coastline with islands, fluoroscope feeling, light things on different level. Collar, belt and belt buckle like a doll or figurine. Colon. Color. Color. Color and shading here is important. Color and shape. Color and shape, hanging in same direction. Color – life blood through them. Color nothing to do with it. Color of green. Color of sky blue. Color splash, streaming down. Colored fireworks, like they look after they've exploded. Colored map. Colored masses, nothing specific; horseshoe crab washing about in waves, sea-green water. Coloring symbolic, that's all it could be. Colossus astride Rhodes. Comes down over other structures, coming down over. Coming up out of the water, things seem to be dragged up with it. Conflict over pelvis fundamental. Confusion, turmoil, just looks like a lot of conflicting forces. Congenial faces, babies with noses, too smart for babies, pulling against each other, both males. Contour of mountains, looking far away, shading. Cotton is generally that shape, I think. Could be a bat or a bird. Could be a butterfly. Could be a butterfly. Could be a couple of clowns with awful funny faces. Could be a leaf, part of a leaf. Could be a meadow. Could be a pair of hunting birds. Could be a statue depicting a toast. Could be a tree. Could be a tree branch with a pair of falcons or birds on it. Could be a woman washing clothes. Could be an anteater head because of the snout. Could be an explosion, everything blown up. Could be an oil drum or gas tank exploding. Could be Bigfoot. Could be curved back, but looks more like a handle that was jutting back rather than just a curve like a headrest. Could be Jell-O. Could be kneeling. Could be old flying animal that lived in prehistoric times, like a bird, bat. Could be some kind of elaborate top or toy mechanism; no idea of what the figures are because they spin so fast. Could be some sort of an emblem like a family crest, it's very colorful. Could be the skull of a person, or an animal.

Could be two tigers climbing up on mountain. Could get little Santa Claus hanging on a Christmas tree. Couple of horses with elongated faces scooting out of thing, look like Picasso horses. Couple of lobsters in some sea grass. Couple of men bowing to each other. Crabs. Craggy dark wood area, irregular formation bare as you see in mountains sometimes. Craggy mountain area. Crawdads. Creatures flying along because of some force. Crocodile head. Cross-section of a cervix. Crudely done face, back with toy pack, color part of idea, color leads to illusion. Crustaceans' ball. Dancers resting on arm, stretched out on floor. Dancers stretched out on floor in costume. Dancing girls, bustles, heads back. Dancing ladies are here. Dark and light areas, the shading. Dark, cloud-like, lot of black, dark moors, weird blowing, thunder and lightning, weird, eerie sounds, element of suspense. Dark gray clouds, just the mass. Dark here and light here. Dark smudges of smoke, all that remains after a heavy fire, like oil burning. Dark spot underneath it, sets off blue. Dead wood of trees, dead wood branches. Deer antlers. Deer antlers, body in flight. Deer in flight. Definitely the abominable snowman, walking on glass, looking at him through the glass, makes his head look far away. Destruction – but they don't really care. Did I say that? Did you ever look at clouds and see things, sort of shapes? Did you make all of these? Different vertebrae, looks like picture in text, color not of living tissue, x-ray study. Distance, darkness and depth, looks heavily wooded, gives depth. Distorting, changing the back light – looking through disturbed water or a fog, either could refract the light enough, I suppose. Do I have to look, it's so scary, oh I can't, it's just big and scary like my nightmares, only I'm not asleep, I just see it all the time trying to crush me,

I can't look at it (*hides head in arms*). Do you have a cat or are you married? Do you see it? Do you want me to say anything else? Dodecanese Islands, a map, association of islands around Turkey and Greece. Doesn't fit into any standard category. Doesn't look like any kind of tool that I've ever seen. Doesn't resemble anything. Dog face with one eye sticking out, something like my dog, this one looks angry. Dog sitting down. Don Quixote was very idealistic. Don't belong to these men. Don't have any temples. Don't know. Don't know 'cause it looks like a butterfly's house. Don't know what it is. Don't know what this is. Don't know why I was thinking of lungs, but there they are. Don't see a lot in that. Don't see anything else. Double bear. Down at the bottom, the darker spot looks like a set of lungs and part of sternum in between them. Down here is the finished road made into a valley – shading makes it look like a road deep in a valley – you're above looking down. Down here's the butterfly, pretty, see, a pretty red one, I like pretty red ones but it's gonna land on this black dirt, it's ugly dirt, it scares me about what will happen to the butterfly. Dragon. Dribbles out into sort of ectoplasm, like baby's round shape, and pug noses, blowing bagpipes. Drooping flowers. Drooping flowers or leaves, looks like dying flowers. Duck's head and neck. Dwarfs or fairies. Each is pulling on it. Each one is defending himself. Eagle to me is a symbol of power and leadership. Eagles' heads. Ear, nose. Ears are back. Ears coming up are rather small. Eiffel Tower seen across a vista of gardens leading to it. Either dueling or something of the sort. Either one of these things sticking up here looks like a piece of meat or bone wrapped in cellophane. Elephants' heads, eyes, trunk. Elephants with big ears. Elongated head. Etching of a fern or a design, it's very pretty. Except for color, gives you an idea of something round and soft. Exploding fireworks. Extended fur is reaching out in some way. Extended trunk, but not feet, cut-off body. Eye here. Eyes and jaws here. Eyes are white, face white, with large lips, nose is set back on camel's head. Eyes, ears, nostrils, looks like animal, incomplete head. Eyes mostly, and upper lip. Eyes, nose, ears; fantastic cat; symbolic/representational, not realistically drawn. Eyes, nose, jowls, hair fluffy, hands, shoulders, bent backwards like this. Eyes of an owl but it is no owl, but probably a Cheshire cat. Eyes on bottom and wings and stinger in back, where it is on fish. Eyes, snout, fur irregular shape, white fur, hooded effect. Eyes, tusks. Face. Face is wide, widens here, makes it look fat. Face, not human, a demon, with ears and horns, eyes, nose, mouth and a tongue. Face of a bird, basket they're carrying. Face of a woman. Face, snout, tail, leg, back, ear. Faith in other people, I think. Fascinating little designs, aren't they? Fear, uncertainty. Feather stuck in hair, eyes, noses. Features look very big and sagged out. Feet here, extended. Female figure diving or swimming, not too clear. Female figure resting. Female genitals, I guess. Female organ. Female sex organs. Fetus, pink color. Field mice. Figure climbing upon incline. Filmy ectoplasm between them, mad at each other but highly interrelated. Finally, a pretty one, it's like a big houseplant, all in bloom, some are beautiful, you should have given me this one before. Fingers. Fire they're warming their hands over is their children burning. Fireworks. Fishes. Fishes. Flags just for decoration. Flags waving in the breeze. Flames. Flowing robes, flying, probably pushed by the wind, could be saints. Flying rabbit with two overbig wings. Foot upraised. For the color, like a pine tree, they're sometimes gray and bluish and there's a cat on each side like they're climbing up, see the legs and the body like a cat (*points*). Forms look like slopes. Forward portion of insect doesn't fit into any standard category. Four large rough rocks piled on top of each other in a special way, like scenic rocks for decorative purposes, or it could be a natural formation. Four legs, no tail, vestigial on one and not existent on the other. Four white spots are just decoration on the shield. From right side up, fireworks. From the distance you see the splashes. From upside down it could be a flower. Gargoyles. Gargoyles in human shape look like in a cathedral, possibly of stone, rough surface of stone, also rounded effect. Gee, a lot of paint. Gee, all I can think of here is a bunch of clouds moving along. General shape and shading. General shape of Italy. General shape of skin and shading, skin over back shaded differently, topside, skin out. Genie's urn. Giant monster towering over someone very small. Girl hanging on a trapeze, leg outstretched up along rope. Girl on a trapeze. Gizzard, laminations. Glow worms. Gnomes, imaginary figures. God, looks like an ape, a raging ape. God of wind like you see in children's books, you see the weird pictures, big blustery thing. Goes all the way up, this whole area looks very irritated and sore. Goes up like a mountain. Goes up; shape. Got four legs. Got legs and a big head shape, got two arms. Got long hat, broomstick, two hands look like end of dust mop, like made of soft material, she is sitting on it and wind is blowing her along. Got their hands together and it looks like they're pushing away. Got their paws, this one's raised. Got themselves angled back, which keeps their faces from being so close together, their heads apart. Got two arms, two big feet. Grasping mouth and jaws, wings out, attacking, predatory. Gray and white matter of spinal cord. Gray fungus mass. Gray metallic helmet with a unicorn peak, to give the appearance of a unicorn. Gray shadows on a field of snow. Gray toy terriers. Green in the center runs into the orange on top and blends with the pink below. Green – never saw green flames but once I did, one little spark. Green reminds me of gall – gall bladder – lower red some muscular formation. Green things decoration. Green things look like menacing ghosts. Green worms with high aspirations considering idealistic matters. Grinning cat face mask, eyes, ears, mouth. Grotesque human figure. Guess that pink could be a bloodstain, dried up. Ha ha, a funny cloud. Ha, that's terrible, it's a very funny picture, I don't think I can tell you about them, it's too awful. Hands outstretched, tall hats, color of devils. Hands pointing with index finger. Happy little clowns looking at each other. Harbor, unusual but possibly like a topographical map, dark is the land. Has a walking stick, bushy hair. Has explosions like fireworks. Has green coat and orange pants on, he's standing. Have a green claw sticking out from arm, I've seen crabs with green claws. Have mound of hair here. Have very rough skin. He has a funny peak to his head and these white eyes, like maybe he's glaring, just staring straight ahead, and he has big bushy sideburns that hang down below his face too, see here are his nostrils (*points*) and his chin is here so they go down below his face; really weird-looking, mean-looking, just staring out like that. He has little arms and these great big boots or something on his feet. He looks mean to me, he's got big ears and he's got his face all scrunched up like he was mad. He looks severe. He smokes a pipe. He was probably a fat man because his hips are broad and he's flattened out a bit more there, see, his little hands are up here, his head looks split open,

I suppose that happens if you're hit by a car and he looks flattened out to me. Head about here. Head and bust. Head and feet. Head and neck of swan. Head and tail. Head and wings, like sleeping. Head, body, hat, balancing hands out. Head, body, legs, they've got on pointed shoes. Head down, maybe grazing, head, wings, haunches of some kind of bull. Head, eyes, long forehead, nose, jowls, beard. Head, face, one person, body here, bow tie, eyes, mouth. Head here, a monument. Head of a bird. Head of a man smoking a pipe. Head of a soft stuffed animal, ears floppy. Head of a teddy bear. Head of a woman, hand over forehead contrasts to white of forehead. Head of alligator with slit eyes. Head of an Indian carved out of rock. Head of elephant, trunk here. Head of stone, looks like a stone monument. Head of two bears here looking up. Head on top. Head on top is real small in comparison to robe. Head or something. Head, shape of wings cut wrong. Head, with cap on, floating around in air. Head with eyes, almost like a ghost. Head with neat features like an otter. Heads and busts, hands outstretched in movement. Heads combined, no bodies, so united, just general feeling, legs dominant, symbolic of sexual organism. Heads drawn back, like ready to crash into each other, ready to do battle. Heads here, they're just this part, the light. Heads strange-shaped, not really pinheads but makes me think of people who put rings on children's heads when young, and put a smaller one on each year 'til it's shaped like this. Heads turned, lips pursed, hair up. Heavy smoke. Heavy smoke, not quite shaped like the A-bomb cloud. Hell, if you don't see it you'd better lock me up and throw away the key, it just looks like that to me, damn it (*throws down card*). Helmet on, sitting back on stool waiting. Here. Here. Here and here. Here are the big wings and the body, it just looks like a bat to me. Here are the hands, something could be crouching with the hands holding up the end. Here are the wings of an eagle. Here at the end, they look like bush roots if you pull 'em out of the ground. Here at the orange and red everything is beautiful. Here at the top, the wings are here and the body part and there's the ditch. Here, chest to chest, slanted back, head down on chest. Here could be a ravine with plateau on two sides. Here I see a profile. Here I see little bugs. Here in the center, you can see the outline of her, these are her hands and legs and hips. Here is a dog, the kind of poodle that has a big ruff around the neck and the body shaved. Here is Santa Claus hurrying along with a tree under his arm. Here is the leg, the rest is some sort of animal. Here is the mouth. Here it is, its tail up. Here it looks like a bottle, kind of. Here it should be hanging down in a pigtail because falling draws it up (*pantomimes with arms as hair*). Here it's black, then white, then black, then the white space, then more black. Here, see the wings are coming across and this is her body part in the middle. Here, see, they're big and round. Here, these are the rays. Here, these right here could be badgers. Here, this is the platform, here, like this. Here within the design I see very faintly something that might be a little mouse. Here's a leaping snake. Here's its head, got an eye, legs, tail, rolled over on its side. Here's mouth, beard. Here's red, pink, blue, orange. Here's the back left foot. Here's the back right. Here's the body and these look like wings. Here's the headmast, is that what they call it? Here's the right paw, left paw. Here's the root or trunk and bush comes down like this, covered with dirt, that's what makes it orange-brown and this is green because it has no sunlight and dirt hasn't reached it and reddish color is from sun burning it, the way the trunk comes down and colors. Here's the wings and body. Here's two horns, and two sets of small horns. He's a chubby guy, see, here's his head and big body and this would be the sax here (*points*), it's narrower at the upper part and then comes to the horn below it. He's a giant spider, like he'll get you too if you don't watch where you walk, and he's got this goat, see the goat got a horn so it must be a goat and he's gonna eat him. He's got a very small head, big cloak that drapes, kind of blowing (*shows with arms*). He's just standing there. He's pounding, grizzly head, this part does not come in. Hey, fireworks. Hey, this is a weird one, like two bears really in a big fight with each other, man, they're hurt too. Hey, you know this part could be a rock. Hey, you know this thing looks like it could be a crowbar like you open crates and things with. Hey, you know this way it reminds me like a toy my daughter has, her grandfather got it for her, it has a couple of rabbits on a teeter-totter and you wind it up and they go up and down, hers isn't gray like this one though. Hind legs of a kitten. Hippopotamus. His arms look like – reminds me of an abominable snowman. His eyes. Hm, it kinda looks like a weird fly, maybe like a horsefly that's pretty big. Hm, looks like a fellow sitting on a stump, maybe a trapper with a big fur coat on stretching out for a rest. Holding cotton candy. Holding up a lot of junk in either hand, not wings, like an old hide of some sort. Horrible bug flying around. Horseshoe crab. Human. Human body and visceral detail. Humpy animal, looks like buffalo. I also see a headless woman crying out for help. I always had a feeling he was a sneaky person, I remember him laying little traps for my mother, makes me feel he was a very alone person. I always wanted to play, but I worked since I was thirteen. I bet they have tartar. I can see the projectiles going. I can't look anymore, it's too frightening, it makes me feel crazy. I can't look or I'll go crazy again. I can't make anything out of all of it, but this lower part looks like a very exotic butterfly. I can't say what else. I can't tell. I can't think of anything else. I couldn't see, that made it even more frightening. I didn't mean the Painted Desert but it's like it, all the colors and the bottom is like the sandstone. I didn't say that, I said a crab with wings, these are the wings, it's a crab, that's all. I didn't say that, you wrote it wrong, it's a whale and see his face there, here's his nose and his chin and his big long body like a whale. I didn't see faces. I don't get much from the white thing, but if I just use this darker part it looks like two dogs rubbing noses. I don't get much out of this one except, you know, this middle red part could be like a clown's mouth, the lips, I'm not sure if you know what I mean, but it could be like you might paint human lips to exaggerate them, that's all though. I don't get too much more out of this one unless it could be a bee too. I don't know. I don't know. I don't know. I don't know. I don't know anything else that comes out of a bottle. I don't know – bitter beetles. I don't know, it looks like some kind of leg like of a person with the toes curled up. I don't know, just a lot of garbage I guess, it doesn't make much sense to me. I don't know, just somebody funny. I don't know, maybe it's a flying squirrel, what do most people see in these things? I don't know much about them, this one is weird 'cause it's got this pointy thing coming out the top, like a stinger, see up here and the rest of it is white like some kind of weird insect. I don't know of any butterflies that go from brown to old rose, butterfly has no head. I don't know the name, it has a special name. I don't know what it's going through, just stuff but it's coming out this side, you can see the path it took, it looks like that to me. I don't know what made me say that. I don't know what made me think of that, I suppose the arch effect, like a cartoon character, when the bowleggedness is over-emphasized like this, you see this is the trunk and these are the skinny legs, they take this stance sometimes. I don't know what made me think of that, maybe I'm hungry, it's just all red like ketchup but you sure don't put it on stone crab. I don't know what the heck they are. I don't know which countries these could be. I don't know why badgers are climbing on it. I don't know why I see Scotties, I don't like them. I don't know why I thought of channel. I don't know why she swallowed the fly, perhaps she'll die. I don't like arguments. I don't like it. I don't like them. I don't like this either, there's another butterfly down here, like getting ready to land on this black part. I don't like this one, it looks like a dead cat. I don't mean his sex but his sign, the ones that are hung (*giggles*) on his shop to let people know what he is, he'll lend you money and things. I don't remember that, I think it must be here a red one, you can see the large leaves. I don't remember what kind of butterfly it is that has large circles on its back, like eyes, makes birds think it's eyes to frighten them off. I don't remember what you call them, gyplane or something, you wrap a string on them and pull and they balance like this for a long time. I don't see anything else though. I don't see it end, it might be any length. I don't see nothin' else there. I don't see the holes for the eyes but the form is right for one. I don't think anything about what I see. I don't think he ever reached it. I don't think I was right. I don't think of them as a teamwork, you know? I don't understand him anymore, he doesn't show things like he used to, he talks about very intellectual things. I feel as if it keeps waving this things, these two winglike arms, helplessly, but it wouldn't do any good. I feel like – I used to feel stronger in my idealism than right now. I feel like I'm a very bitter person, the square butterfly looks like a bitter butterfly. I feel like it could be disintegrated or blown away. I felt it was phony. I felt it was very humiliating. I get a general impression of all kinds of squirmy animals. I get the impression of something from Greek mythology, like a woman standing there, like a goddess with smoke or fog on each side, that's all I see. I get the impression of two animals like billy goats or deer butting their heads, like they do in a mating struggle. I got a beating for it, I was jealous of the cat getting more attention than I did. I got a feeling of feet upright. I guess he's not very friendly, if someone took his head off. I guess I'd say a hawk, see the big wings and these here are the feet that can grab things easy when they are out looking for prey, they have these really sharp claws. I guess it could also be an insect, has claws to grab. I guess it could be a couple of African women pulling an animal apart. I guess it could be a wolf kinda growling. I guess it's an island and this part is like a harbor, you know. I guess it's supposed to be a symbol of strength, but not for me, are fearful, ruthless birds. I guess I've been playing *Dungeons and Dragons* too long. I guess the blue thing could be spiders too. I guess the – it's just the whole thing. I guess the square of 'em with rough edges. I guess this center part could be a crab or something like a crab. I guess underneath the gray birds' legs, looks like eyes, V, like camel's face with V being nose. I guess you could call it that. I had earaches, eye infections. I had strange communications with him, I thought he was diabolical. I hated that cat, I tried to flush him down the toilet, I once threw him out a four-story window, he landed on someone's face, and the guy came up to our apartment all bloody. I have a tendency to think I'll get – I'll always end up with the short end of the stick. I heard somewhere if you see that stuff you're preoccupied with it, is that right? I held the card right side up. I hope not, no one should see that, it's the huge thing here and the rest is her. I just can't say, it's too awful. I just generally think of the story, they were OK because they were passed over. I just get the feeling from this part. I just had a funny thought. I just inferred it. I just respond in terms of a touching quality. I just see the head; he is puffing hard on the cigarette. I know I should try to make something of it. I know what that looks like. I like flowers and I see some tulips here, yellow tulips. I like it better like this, now that's a bird, like an eagle zooming up. I like this color, there's a map there, like islands. I mean explosion, I never heard of a implosion, I mean explosion, see, like it's all going up (*gestures with hands*) and this orange is like the fire part when that happens, I didn't say implosion though, explosion, that's what I said. I mean ribs, and all of that, see, some of it is in pairs, like the things that we have two of, like the lungs and things. I meant to identify the portion. I never had a dog but we couldn't have one at the parish. I never liked the smell of it. I never saw a brilliant red butterfly. I never saw any white insects like this one but I guess they must be somewhere. I really don't know if it looks like one the more I look at it. I really don't know what it is, but I said two people 'cause you could stretch your mind to think that like here is the head and the bodies and the arms, just down at their sides, like they're just facing each other, you know, like looking at each other, but not really doing anything. I said that? I said that? I saw a movie with a black widow spider biting a guy, he died. I saw colored pictures like that, like a stomach or your sides. I saw definite lines. I saw it like his head, the monster that is, but if you look just separate it looks like a rock. I saw the sheep when I held the card upside down. I see a face – very elongated – like Egyptian carved figure, eyes and nose, peculiar coiffure, carved in stone. I see a rabbit, two rabbits, one on each side, they're looking at each other. I see an exotic flower. I see flags, two flags, they are green and waving. I see some roots out here. I see that all the time, the shading and color. I see the eye. I see two dogs' heads here. I seem to associate bats with some kind of terror. I slept by myself, I was afraid. I suppose I could see a design like a sculpture that might be on a building with the gargoyles on the sides. I suppose it could be a butterfly, it's rather torn though, like it was decaying. I suppose it could be a mashed, cracked, squashed crab. I suppose it could be a moth too, with its wings out like it was flying, but not with these side parts out here. I suppose it looks like different kinds of moths or insects, I'll say a butterfly. I suppose it's the color, it all looks like intestines opened up. I suppose that the center could be a man who has been run over, very gruesome, I don't care for that. I suppose that the upper part could be a butterfly but I can't make anything out of the pink. I suppose the center could be a bell. I suppose the entire thing could be a butterfly. I suppose the orange things could be deer. I think I have a one-track mind because this center red could also be a mask like you might wear at a costume ball. I think if you cut these parts away (*points*) you could think of it as a fountain, see, this top would be the peak and the rest is just the sculpted work, except the white, they would be lights. I think it could be a woman standing in the middle there. I think it looks like a cat but I'm not sure. I think my guts look like that. I think of a ruthless and insane monster who goes completely out of control and destroys people. I think that could be a womb in the center when you look this way it has fluid in it, maybe a placenta. I think that's all. I think that's blood running out of this bug at the top of the poor bug. I think that's what they look like, I've never seen one but they're all black and fuzzy like this one. I think the bigger part could be an animal skin, like a blanket or rug. I think they were in lots of fights with other dogs. I think woodpeckers are very silly. I thought I saw them at night. I thought it was a different one. I thought of a butterfly but they usually have bigger wings, it could be a moth though, it's black like a moth flying around. I told you it was awful, vulgar, it makes me sick to look, see them; I can't look anymore. I try to do what I can at work, everyone tells me that I do a good job, but others don't care, and they end up with better deals. I used to be afraid to go to bed, they'd bite me on the throat. I used to play a game in which I was an Indian, I remember telling my mother about the game, it was like giving my inner self to her, she just didn't react. I used to see aerial maps like this in the army. I want to be left alone. I want to forget about them, not to let them be part of my life. I was always afraid of ghosts, bogeymen, etc. I was really very disgusted and completely humiliated. I wasn't really thinking of a top, but a gyroscope, you know you pull the string and they stay balanced like this because they spin a long time, it's a pretty good shape of one, just the white area. I watched spiders at work, they would catch a fly, tie him up and – I watched him with a praying mantis, we let him loose. I wonder who drew these pictures, they're really hard to make out, I suppose it could be two people having their hands together. Ice cream, cone, shadow. Icicles. I'd like to see two women do anything together (*laughs*). I'd say it looks like to me some kind of flying insect. I'd say that's just a lotta fog. I'd say these are a couple of wolves climbing a tree. I'd say this is two guys who are fighting about something, you know, when I look this way it's like them pictures of the bad black lung disease, these here are the lungs, one here and one here (*points*). If a chicken could stretch its neck so far. If I did something wrong – would be as if was banned. If I just look at the face part and these little parts here it reminds me of a big hairy bird, it's separate from the monster and if you look at these lines it looks like a lot of hair. If I just look at this brown spot I can make out like a deer jumping there, there's one here too. If I look at it differently I see two people but they have the bodies of bears. If I look this way the pink part could be an umbrella. If I turn it again, like this, the upper part could be mountains I suppose, is that OK? If I turn it this way it could be a butterfly, the same part, but the tail of the moth would now be the antennae of the butterfly, it could be gliding or floating. If I turn it this way it looks like a couple of big old maple trees off on a hill. If I turn it this way it looks like an explosion up here, like flames coming out. If I turn it this way it reminds me of a dog's head, like a dog with the flat nose I can't remember, oh yeah, a Scottie. If in color it would be beautiful; this is a negative of a photograph. If it doesn't have to be something really identical, you could see this as people at a party. If it was mine, I wouldn't keep it in a container. If it's that difficult why bother? If the end parts are eliminated it might be a moth. If the robe was closed, you couldn't see the people or feet because the robe goes to the floor. If you just take the top, it looks like a mountain, you know like a big volcano or big mountain of some sort. If you just take the top part it could be an Indian chief with his arms spread out and he's got feathers on his arms, like an Indian costume. If you look down you see a man in flight, sort of a Leonardo da Vinci learning how to fly. If you look just at this top part it reminds you of a TV antenna. If you really use all of it, like the white part too, it is like a modern design pottery. If you spill milk and leave it, it makes spots like on this floor, and see the mosquito is there and he's going to eat the milk up, they're dangerous 'cause they eat holes in things. If you turn it this way it looks like a floral display, it's quite pretty with the different-colored flowers organized into a display, like on a head table at a banquet or something. If you turn it this way this part looks like a seal, it looks like he's honking for food or something. If you turn it upside down, it looks like a very angry person, with big eyes. If you turn it upside down like this the center looks like a mushroom. I'll be damned! I'm afraid of them. I'm always a witch on Halloween; I wish I could paint my cat all black for Halloween. I'm happy for him, see he's flying again, right there, don't look at the other part though. I'm looking at it different now, just the top and these would be the feathers on his costume like a ceremonial robe and he has his arms stretched out like calling or signaling. I'm not so sure it's a seal because there's a paw, looks like it's black and slippery. I'm not sure exactly why it looks like that, I suppose the shape of it just reminds me of a bell, like a church bell. I'm not sure if they're men or women but they're black like African people and I guess that's what reminds me of cannibals and they're pulling on this thing I don't know what it is. I'm not sure of the name, but they have a shell that goes in the center like this one does and they have these spikes coming out here. I'm not sure they're correct but they look like that sort of map. I'm sorry but that's all I can see here. I'm taking dancing lessons, there are two boys I'm interested in. I'm using just the orange part now, and it looks like two witch things, they're not real witches, but like cartoons of them. Images of Don Quixote. Imperial German, eagle type. Impression of black on black and particularly because the eye is glowing. In battle dress, like dueling (*imitates posture*). In between the people, a moth or butterfly, but upside down. In distance and beyond is pink flower-bed. In form of chess piece resting on little stand, it is carved, you can see the highlights. In irrational flight – this seems half-witted too. In middle is a woman holding her hands over her head, sort of a grotesque type, like a Balinese dancer. In some ways, looks like all four legs are spread out. In those books them Indians have buffalo hides hanging on their teepee and that's what it looks like. Incense. Indian profile, outline of nose and strong jaw. Indian snake charmers. Indian totem design. Insect with antennae flying with back to us, long legs. Insects grabbing other insects and devouring them. Inside, skeletons are always inside, that's obvious. Instead of looking inward, look outward at each other, an evil thing to do, they're looking at each other's actions so they can operate. Interested in what happens when you mix colors in painting, the intricate effect of black and red superimposed as contrasted to black and red above. Is this gonna take long? It ain't always easy to come by. It can be avoided. It could all be a cat's face too, it's white and gray. It could also be an airplane flying in a storm, it must be a weather plane, yes of course, they do that. It could be a bat too, it's all black, it could be one I suppose, that's all though. It could be a butterfly too. It could be a cell under a microscope, like when they are magnified, like separating like they do all the time. It could be a leaf too, a dead leaf, all curled up. It could be a man's head too, it's like a side view, you know, just like an old man maybe with a beard too, one here too. It could be a negative picture of a woman's face, the black shows her light-colored hair. It could be a tree, a pine tree, but you have to discount these little parts out here. It could be a woman with her hat perched way forward. It could be an old tree too, I don't know what kind, big though. It could be an x-ray of the inner ear, I remember those from biology too, they caught this one as it was vibrating you can see the tremors of it by the way it is extended on each side. It could be like a flower too that is opening up, not really moving but like a picture took of a flower when it was opening, like the time kind of photography. It could be like a volcano erupting too with all the fire shooting up. It could be stained glass, like a window that's being put together, a lot of pieces have been selected to give the right color and tone effect. It could be the Fourth of July, like fireworks exploding. It could even look like a cat's face, at least this part here, there's two of them and they have their paws together. It could really be either but I'll say butterfly, OK? It couldn't possibly be anything else. It does look like that but a little melted like the flavors ran together, mixed together, you could think of sherbet more than ice cream. It does look like that, you see the head here and the body, I don't know what kind but they have little ears and noses. It doesn't have any philosophical meaning, it just is, it just exists. It doesn't look like much this way, it could be two bushes up on a small hill. It doesn't show the chair at all, except for the extension, the shawl covers the chair, this blanket here, looks like they have something draped over their laps. It don't look like much, maybe a woman there in the middle but she doesn't have a head. It even has the oil tankers. It fit over his head, would wear it to frighten us, he was kidding around. It gave me the feeling of massive animals. It goes straight down here to the feet. It goes up making almost a circle around it (*points*). It has a magic point on the top, like to make things happen when you don't know they will, and a little trunk, magic trees always have a little trunk. It has a white forehead and a gray chin and whiskers and the eyes are not so clear but they're right here, it's a pretty good cat's face. It has all of these lines, the shading effect which makes it all look furry to me, it really doesn't have much shape like anything, like a coat or something, just a piece of fur. It has all the different colors like it was in full bloom, my mom has some like it, see the different parts, the petals are pink and some blue and this is the pot. It has different colors mixed like sandstone. It has feet. It has that outline, the hips and the legs and the upper part and these might be her hands raised as if she's just standing there. It has that shape to it with the little seedpods on the ends, like an inverted V, you know what I mean? It has that V shape to it, like the antennae that are built into the sets, or I think you can buy them separate, they just have this shape. It has the big wings and it's multi-colored, pink and orange and the colors tend to intermix, that's the way they do on the prettier butterflies, the colors aren't sharply defined but mix together like this, it's pretty. It has the big wings and the body part here in the middle, I think they are shaped like this although I've never seen one up close, and I hope I don't. It has the form to it, but it should be colored, they make them in such beautiful colors, but it does have the form. It has the head and the whiskers, and it does look furry and it's all flat like it had been squashed, see, the legs are way out to the side. It has the wings and the claws out front like it was attacking, you know charging something, they swoop down and grab things with their claws. It has the wings out like it was flying along and the narrow body, I guess like a dragonfly rather than a housefly because of the narrow body, houseflies have a fatter body than this. It has these pincher-type things and looks like legs. It has wings, big wings (*yawns*), it's terrible, all black, it's making me depressed again, like I'll lose my mind looking at it, it even shows the little feelers up here on the body. It is a caricature, ludicrous. It is fluffy. It is lying down, crouching on front legs. It is one of those chinless people. It is out of proportion. It is the darker red portion. It just all looks furry, the shades there. It just has that form, like a vase, see (*points*). It just has that shape to it, like a golf tee, it really looks like that, see the point here and here it's bigger where you put the ball. It just has that shape to it, see these are the longer things like they have on them, it really looks a lot like they do. It just is and the dirt is down below, if it's flying the dirt must be below. It just kinda gives that impression if you use your mind a little. It just looks like features, not a whole head. It just looks like it could be an island and this part could be the harbor, you know like where ships go to keep away from a storm or bad weather. It just looks like one to me, it has that form to it, like a big mountain. It just looks like one to me, the way it's shaped there. It just looks like two people with their hands together, I really don't know what made me think of that. It just reminds me of that, see the ponytail and the forehead and nose and chin, like they're just looking at you. It looks as though it is so highly polished light is reflected off it. It looks like a bug collection with a lot of kinds of bugs mounted in an attractive pattern. It looks like a little animal I studied in biology, pigmented body, two eye spots. It looks like a mask, a horror mask. It looks like a very formal party, rather colorful with the decorations around. It looks like a whale to me, see here. It looks like ink spilled on a piece of paper. It looks like it's inside the bush, see it's a different color here so it's higher up the bush, see it? It looks like it's ready to alight on a flower. It looks like mud to me. It looks like shoes right there and these look like their arms and this looks like the cauldron. It looks like some kind of a skin, maybe a bearskin like a trophy you put up on a wall. It looks like somebody put ink on a piece of paper and folded it together. It looks like the faces of two pigs in here. It looks like there's an angel there if you could see her better you could see the gold and silver on her dress, she has her arms out like this (*demonstrates*) sort of like she's getting ready to fly but she's not yet. It looks like those were the arms. It looks like two antennae and the wing span and the little tail. It looks like two little girls, with big ponytails, see the nose and chin and this would be the shoulders here. It looks like two people cooking something in this big kettle. It looks like two people with their wings against each other, hooded figures waving to each other. It looks like two spiders up here. It looks like two witches praying by putting their hands up against each other instead of putting their hands together. It looks pushed out, all of the colors there make it look more round, pushed outward as muscles do when flexed sternly. It looks the way it is in the market, packaged in cellophane. It might be a bush too, like a little plant, in a planter. It might be an x-ray of something, I guess. It might be undersea coral. It must be Christian because the arms are out like the crucifixion and it's on this flagpole. It must be dead or nearly dead because it has lost so much blood, all this here and here, the poor thing, it was probably a nice bug. It probably has nothing to do with this. It reminds me of my mother, to tell the truth. It seems like it would be dead to be like this, it's all dark and it's ragged at the edges, like some of the wings had already fallen off through the decaying process. It seems so big. It shows a woman standing with her arms out and light radiating around her. It was when he was really small, before he was old enough to work it himself, and it had a stand like this one and so you'd make it go and set it in the stand, see the white is the top and the stand would be down in here (*traces*). It's a black and white one like you see sometimes. It's a butter churn, yeah, a churn. It's a butterfly with its hands out like it's ready to fight. It's a collision of rain clouds, thunder, it's probably the same one I saw before but now in a collision. It's a combination of a woman and a bat or insect. It's a difficult problem. It's a giant foot, no, wait, erase that, it's a giant man with a giant foot, man he's a big one. It's a giant jellyfish too like he's sitting down on this post. It's a giant's face, looking right at me and I don't like it, it's mean-looking. It's a map of two big islands, I can't remember the name but I used to know. It's a moth, a gray moth. It's a stingray. It's a terrible black butterfly, you don't see them very often, it's very, very ugly, it makes me nervous, the way it's flying around there. It's a weird bird, like it has this beak and a really hairy face and small wings like hunched up just in a big hairy ball. It's all different colors like when they explode outward to form a pattern like this, like a rocket going off, it makes a pretty pattern. It's all furry-looking (*rubs card*).

It's all I know, it's just kind of splattered out. It's all in gray, it's got different shades, swatches and swirls give a gauze-like appearance, sort of a spectral type, doesn't have hands or feet. It's also a plain inkblot. It's an accident. It's as if she's propped up in the stirrups and would be seeing herself in a mirror or something, inspecting her genitals for signs of cancer. It's better this way, it's like a flag, a Christian flag made from the hide of a cat. It's dark like clouds but it's funny too 'cause it goes around in a half circle, like part is missing. It's flat on some white surface. It's fuzzy like that and this shading gives the effect of it, could be any shape. It's going out. It's gold. It's got a head like a bat, legs like a crane or bat, behind when flying, wings like a bat, not smooth, but ribbed. It's got big wings and big hands like he's reaching out to grab something like maybe he's ready to fight, see the hands are here. It's got the prongs up here and it has that general body shape to it, like a crab (*points*), see, here. It's got the triangular face of a deer, flared back out by nostrils (*points*). It's got the wings way out and it's like going up 'cause the head is out to see where it's going. It's grinning in ridicule. It's inside a body, like blood spurting out of your veins. It's interesting. It's, it's vulgar, it's two men peeing. It's just all gooey-looking as if they stepped on it so you can see the claws up here but the shell is all squashed and crashed up. It's just like a mountain range might look. It's just round like one. It's just the whole thing. It's just their tops and they've got their noses together, that's how they kiss. It's just this here, just straight. It's just two heads of people, they look sort of old to me, like adults. It's kinda long and the shape. It's like a brush burn or a fire-created burn, pink and orange, like the skin is not there anymore and just the fleshy part is exposed, ugh. It's like a crab with some wings too. It's like a glass bowl with a top on it, like a pretty candy dish or something, it's very round. It's like two Lucys, from *Peanuts*, she's always bouncing around and her hair goes up like this, this looks like she's dancing away in front of the mirror watching herself, Lucy would do something like that, see her nose and her arm is out and it's like she is bent sort of at the waist, like cartoons do but real people can't do that. It's no good anymore though, it's all beat-up and dirty. It's no longer red, it's pink, like a smear for a blood-count test or something. It's not a very pleasant thought, but I think it does look like that. It's not all that good, but you can see it, here are the eyes and nose and a little mouth, it's kind of a narrow face, weird-looking. It's not finished, dug out of a hill. It's not got as much the shape of the shell as the clear patterns of markings. It's not much more pleasant this way, it looks like a big bat. It's not really the entire dogs, you can only see them from the waist up, just their shoulders and heads and it's like they're being playful the way dogs rub noses when they play, see, here are the noses touching and the rest of the head and so on. It's not the kinda thing I care about for my own house but you see them other places, like a museum, they're supposed to mean something, see, a head on each side kinda pointed outward. It's real thick here, at top flourished like an Indian decoration. It's really strange but better than the others, it's a scared animal, scared out of his wits, he's jumping across all of these things and seeing himself do it down here in the water. It's really two people, women I would think, but they have huge bear bodies, that's really unusual. It's really two pinheads in a circus playing patty-cake. It's red, everybody knows that. It's right in the middle with his ears up here. It's round, has shading and light in the front. It's so ugly I can't look. It's something that crawls, like an ant, it could get on you and bite you, the big ones are so scary, one bit me once, they can fly. It's sort of a grayish blue, not like the other gray like for the moths. It's stomping a tree down. It's the head, see the eyes and the mouth here and the way the white goes up it's like he was growling and his ears are sticking out too, like when an animal gets mad his ears go out like that. It's the Painted Desert. It's the same idea as the butterfly, but you could see it like a bee too, with the wings and head and feet. It's the same part but reversed, but it looks like it's flying whereas the moth doesn't. It's the screwing, just like on the other one, here's the penis and it's going all the way through her as if it was almost coming out her rear. It's the tongue drooling. It's too dark here to see features. It's unusual to see that. It's very clear, this (*points*) is the penis and she is open, yes. It's very colorful, like a butterfly might be and you could imagine the orange parts as the out parts of the wings and the green would be the fuller parts of the wings, I don't know, I just thought of a butterfly, it's so colorful. It's very much like an animal mask of some sort, like a dog or cat. It's yellow, we learned about that in school, so if it's yellow it's Chinese blood. I've always been resentful that I wasn't playing. I've had two teeth pulled recently. I've heard a lot about this test but I didn't realize how gruesome it was. I've never watched sex occur but this is what it must look like, you can see the penis and she is exposed. I've read in his pictures, people flying, looks to me like they're falling, falling towards big red butterfly in middle. I've seen dead trees, that's the way they look, their branches droop, everything is sloping towards the ground. I've seen them and they do look like this, with the dark colors and the bright colors, this one happens to have some reds that join in with the blacks, I think they call them preemies, yes preemies. I've seen them on the side of the road. Jackrabbit. Jagged edges, I've seen pictures, enter in here, walls and empty area. Jaw out, foreleg coming out, rushing out at great speed, almost horizontal. Jean-Paul Sartre – hell is other people. Jeez, I guess it could be another bearskin, just the bottom part. Jumping. Just a bone. Just a bunch of junk, like trash and garbage piled up there, all different kinds of things, all this down here looks rotted. Just a mass of color, could be a coat of arms or an ad of something. Just all bunches up there. Just color and shape, don't know what it comes from. Just color decoration. Just conflict in general. Just decoration. Just glancing, a bat. Just – I like lights, and I like color, I like a flame because it looks like it has so much life, a mysterious thing. Just I'm not as different as I thought I was, I can relate to people better than I used to. Just like two flags, like they cross them sometimes, see they're square like two flags. Just little extensions here, shaped like ones I've seen in parks. Just looks like one. Just looks like one. Just looks that way. Just people that I don't like. Just plain tissue paper. Just plain worms. Just scales. Just see heads, they are looking up. Just seems that way. Just seems that way, these could be the wings. Just shape. Just some red symmetrically arranged, doesn't look like anything. Just that it's part of a female. Just the emphasis of the center line and the emanations. Just the light gray part, ladies' hands. Just the quality of a negative, shading, but doesn't look like anything. Just the red, oh, it's awful. Just the shape. Just the word fly. Just the word 'monkeys'. Just their red behinds, ugly sort of thing. Just this center (*points*) section, it looks as if the intestine or something had been opened up and you can see in it. Just this here. Just this part (*points*), it could be an old jacket or something. Just this part (*points*) the line here is darker so it would be the canal and then it comes up, see, it gets lighter (*shows with hands*). Just two eyes cut into something. Just when I was in elementary school, wishing there really was one. Just whiskers. Keeps getting lighter, squirting water. Kerosene lamp with a stand down here. Kidneys. Kidneys don't curve like that, also not adrenal glands but associate that shade with kidneys and kidneys with glands. Kidneys or adrenal glands. Kind of like a stingray too, only tail's not skinny enough. Kind of shaped like feathers. Kinky black bear with no head, shaggy bear. Knees here, with shawls. Knock-kneed kid standing here holding up a furry set of wings. Lady at a costume ball as some insect. Lake in white part, eroded down, just edge. Lambs' blood over the door. Land formation like France with English channel. Land is gray. Large eyes, teeth. Large foreheads, snub noses, chins, body not well-formed. Leaves falling down to earth. Leering face of a pirate, a weird head. Left is a light eye. Legs are outside lighter gray, head that of a half-wit, these might be his arms. Legs are too long to be proper, would have to chop here. Legs, body shape, and has two heads like this. Legs, nose, standing on something. Legs of ballet dancer on her toes, tights on. Legs of woman with heavy thighs coming down. Length and shape. Leprechauns looking at each other with certain amount of malice but ectoplasm between them so they are related even if they don't like each other. Let me study it, ah, two crabs fighting to get at a wishbone, see this is the wishbone here it's split in two ends. Let's skip this one, I don't know what it might be. Light and dark rain clouds. Light and dark sort of separates hair from face, either in shadow or black women with lighter hair, which is what suggested since it's gray. Light from above would make a shadow. Light part is eyes, Rudolph type of nose, sticks out. Light rays are here. Light shining from on top. Like a bone you would see in a desert. Like a cockatoo, large, sharp beak, body, facing away. Like a collie. Like a falcon, wings up forward, here a sharp beak, tuft of feathers on head. Like a fantasy I'd have in childhood; rabbits are happy, little, perky creatures. Like a parachute dropping earthward; something seems to be attached to it. Like a picture of a storm, black and gray, coming there in waves, storm over the sea. Like a ritual, the way they hold hands up, hair is fuzzy and dark, have whitish whiskers and thick lips. Like a river. Like a shield. Like a skeleton. Like a snake could rise up but not on the tip of its tail, but this way sort of can lean against each apparatus, have more support. Like a spinning top. Like a touch-me-not. Like a tulip with orange petals and the green leaves around it and it's planted in the kind of soil that they cover with colored stones like this pink could be crushed bricks or something. Like big blue lobsters that can eat you up, they have them some places and they can get you with all the big legs and claws, they're terrible, I can't look, it's too scary, it makes me depressed. Like Chinese animals, scorpion. Like everything ascending from hell below. Like if you tear up an animal it all looks this way, kind of bloody on the outside parts and bony insides with all the parts. Like Panama in dark part in center. Like parrots, dark chest, beak, white eyes and belly. Like picture in an anatomy book, colors too. Like – smoke comes up, like in the movies, to guard it, makes the area safe. Like tentacles reaching out for food, fur is reaching out for something from the atmosphere. Like they have little bits of fur on them like in here (*points*) and they are black and have these big kinda legs. Like they're trying to keep as far away as they can. Like thorns on an animal or life in the sea, with thorns to protect itself. Like two birds, blue birds, I suppose. Like two people, like one robe because these legs aren't big enough. Like with their legs, like I bounce on a couch with my bottom. Like you've cut the poor critter in half. Little animals falling through the air with their tails streaming behind them. Little dog, whole body, like when held up in arms and it's kicking. Little paws, noses up, texture of fur. Little tall hats, faces sticking out playfully. Lobster claw. Lobsters – claws and color – may not have nails like that. Long black evening gloves. Long ears. Long lower lip, the mouth with protruding lips. Long nose, little eyelash, mouth, neck, chest – from then on indistinct – frowsy hair like French poodles but this is a setter's face. Long tail. Long tail, shape only. Look like clouds but vaguely remind me of a profile of a head. Look – oh – looks like an alligator. Looking down into a chasm. Looking down on something, here a dam and here is the land formation, like a bridge across here, like those moving railroad bridges and this is the platform in the middle of the river. Looking high up and reading. Looking very angry, arms out and up. Looks a little like a carrot except not the right color. Looks as if you're standing on top of a very large object, looking down into a chasm. Looks exactly like one body and wings. Looks kinda like a monarch butterfly, but it doesn't have markings like they do. Looks like a bat. Looks like a bat. Looks like a bat, but it's got antennae, bats don't have antennae. Looks like a bee. Looks like a blackbird with a hole cut in it. Looks like a bow tie in the middle. Looks like a bush. Looks like a butterfly. Looks like a butterfly except colors are wrong. Looks like a butterfly with long wings. Looks like a cat sitting up on its haunches with head all the way up and his whiskers up there. Looks like a cavern. Looks like a cloud that you see that seems to look like something – this could be some kind of bird. Looks like a clown with a pretty flattened-out head, somebody hit him. Looks like a dancer with very fat legs, pigeon-toed and knock-kneed and big costume. Looks like a dissection; parts of intestines. Looks like a fire or explosion in a city by the water and reflection in water, lot of smoke and fire. Looks like a forest scene reflected in water in autumn. Looks like a fountain in the back. Looks like a funny-book page. Looks like a goose looking in the mirror. Looks like a lady looking in a mirror. Looks like a lady with a big head. Looks like a lamppost or a light. Looks like a little pig. Looks like a map of Italy, shadings show mountains and terrain. Looks like a mask my father used to have, a red rubber mask. Looks like a maze of sea animals, crabs, spiders. Looks like a monster. Looks like a person standing on top of a hill of some sort, dressed as some sort of bird, like an Indian. Looks like a picture I saw recently. Looks like a picture of a colon. Looks like a picture taken right there. Looks like a series of masks rising from smoke, two women, dwarfs or goblins and smoke. Looks like a shell I once found. Looks like a snowy mountain. Looks like a spider. Looks like a wall that has been shot with a cannon and red-like blood from people who got killed. Looks like a wizard or monk or something. Looks like a wizard with a big, long robe (*moves arms out imitating robe*) getting ready to cast some evil spell, looks like something they'd put in children's cartoons (*pushes card back*). Looks like an x-ray of somebody's insides. Looks like animal with bushy tail, squirrel or something like that. Looks like apes, shaped like apes; has the red like fire. Looks like bear's heads, except that the ears are thrown back too far, like young bears. Looks like caterpillars climbing up a tree. Looks like clouds. Looks like clouds floating along. Looks like egg yolks dropped down. Looks like fans here and these look like people down here. Looks like fantastic gargoyles on a fifteenth-century building. Looks like four wings, body, different-colored wings, mounted. Looks like girls playing with one another with hands out over there. Looks like grass. Looks like he's sucking the other one in. Looks like inside of your body. Looks like it has butterfly wings. Looks like it is a section of scales of some kind, shading makes it look like that. Looks like it would feel rough and furry, that is the major impression. Looks like it's taking off, because these are all spread out and that looks like fire coming out. Looks like it's trying to get away. Looks like lambs jumping. Looks like Mephistopheles with horns and feet ensconced in a flowing cape. Looks like nervous system. Looks like on the back, the two red marks, the upper torso of an otter, hanging upside down. Looks like pastel colors, just the color quality. Looks like ready to go after something. Looks like reefs – coral reefs. Looks like some x-ray picture of something, light and dark shadows in it. Looks like sort of shoes of some sort. Looks like that's a bat with a frog head or something. Looks like the bone from an animal. Looks like the entrance to a castle, and the red things look like something symbolic. Looks like the face of a rhinoceros or something. Looks like the frame of the body, the chest, the stomach, the ribs and the tubes running into the lungs. Looks like the grain of shell. Looks like the Gumps, talking maybe, but like something added for a little color. Looks like the heart and the ribs and all. Looks like their heads are touching and their hands are touching. Looks like there's something destructive about these two figures. Looks like they got their hands and them look like chickens. Looks like two animal figures: bears on symbolic coat of arms. Looks like two bears climbing up a mountain. Looks like two dogs up here. Looks like two eyes and nose right there and that looks like a mouth. Looks like two hands, looks like wings, a wingspan. Looks like two horses – shape – got four legs. Looks like two men holding a package and putting it down. Looks like two people together with a bow tie in the middle of them or something. Looks like two people, with another person in the middle with hands held up, like that (*pantomimes, hands held up alongside head*), a double-headed person. Looks like two persons facing one another. Looks like two waiters bowing to one another, either that or they are trying to carry something. Looks like two witches dancing, they got hands and legs up like that, got hats on, got black coats. Looks like umbilical cords coming out of the babies' mouths, only one has eyes open, other has eyes closed. Looks like x-ray showing spots in the lungs, there is a lack of clarity. Looks more like a bow – has no butterfly. Looks more porous than the heart, the color too, the pocket-like shape. Looks something like the distance. Looks sort of like there's two sort of mole-like animals on the side. Looks sort of old, sort of decaying, pieces falling off, either dirt or decomposing, something dead. Looks upside-down because it seems that generally the wings of butterflies are larger on top. Lots of color design in here. Lovely green evening dress lying ready to be worn, skirt spread so it won't get crushed. Makes me think of ballerinas who I think are really beautiful women. Makes me think of myself right now. Makes me think of myself, when I was growing up, entering puberty, my breasts weren't developing, I felt insecure about it, even up until recently, I felt I wasn't completely a woman. Makes me very sad because I used to feel that I understood him. Man. Man in dark suit with white shirt, standing with hands in his pockets, indefinite head, shirt is white and comes down to point where coat is open. Man is in middle and other parts are the wings which belong to the man; gives you feeling of power, as if man can fly. Man, that's a bat, a black bat. Man, these are weird, I guess it could be some kind of insect there in the middle. Man, with a very bushy beard, large mouth. Man's foot, sticking up, might be a man in there but don't really see it. Man's head. Man's nose, his arms, his feet, silly hat on top and this might be something he's sitting on. Map of area, the shapes. Map of countries with interconnecting waterways. Map of Italy. Map with areas built up to give altitude, fluoroscopic feeling from the different shades. Markings on bark – tropical trees – with extensions. Mask, cat face. Masses of storm clouds. May be the smoke left from some kind of explosion. Maybe a Christmas tree, it has all the different colored lights on. Maybe a cloud formation like at night, it's all dark and it's like moving up, all billowy like when you look up sometimes at night and see the clouds, they seem to move fast. Maybe a strange-looking bottle opener. Maybe a waterfall back in a valley or gorge. Maybe an animal penis, monkey. Maybe butterflies are blind. Maybe if I just use the head of the monster it looks like something else, like a flower, yes, that's better. Maybe, I'm not sure. Maybe it's an ecology party or something like that. Maybe not rocking chairs – wheelchairs, they've got handles to push. Maybe reclining on a hillside. Maybe section of some country. Maybe some kind of donut with a hole in the middle. Maybe that could be a top or not a top but a thing you pull with a string and it goes fast and balances for a long time, my sister had one once. Maybe they're toys that are stuck and one is broken off at the head. Maybe umbrella tree, doesn't look like that, I never saw one. Medical charts, part of an anatomical chart. Men dressed up in evening dress, face, noses, eyes; swerving back; the bandstand below in front and decorations or the theater on side. Men pulling away from each other, dress seen, neck supposed to be here and these are her hands. Menstruation. Middle and sides dark, edges light as though pulled; furry side is up, spotted, perhaps a leopard's fur, that isn't very furry, is it? Middle looks like a figure without a head, with a belt. Middle part looks like some kind of urn. Middle section looks like an umbrella tree. Might be. Might be a plume for a woman's hat. Might be a representation of a woman decidedly knock-kneed, ridiculous headdress, maybe practicing for beaux-arts ball. Might even be a mask. Miserable. Mists are grayish-blue. Monkey up in a tree looking down, tail hanging down, feet here. Monkeys in the zoo. Monster. Moose's head. More like a silhouette. More like child's or elf's, round, upturned nose, eyes. Mostly an interesting study in gray. Mostly the color, some sort of underwater flowering plant. Mostly the shape. Mottling of same areas, looks like something magnified as though of different transparencies under a microscope, eyes, ears, big open jaws and mandible coming out. Mountain and snow, reflected in water. Mountains in the distance, seems so far away, especially the top part. Moustache drooping down makes it look sad or drugged. Mouthpiece like a trumpet, against lips, might be blowing out or breathing. Mud. Multicolored inkblot. Mushroom-type chef's hats (*outlines whole dog with finger*). My father (*laughs*).

My goodness, this is an owl sitting on a dead tree and staring right at you. My mom got it for me and at first I liked it but then I thought it was too big, I don't remember what ever happened to it but I think I lost it, see it bows out here and here (*points*). My mother had some we used to look at years ago. My mother reminds me of a washerwoman, she's very subservient, simple, she works very hard and doesn't get anything from it, just enough to sustain herself. My, oh, my! My older brother. My parents. My parents not being enough support to him now and I'm not now; in a way that's my fault, in a way not. My, that's ugly, it looks like a man and a woman, as if he's doing something to her, actually he's inside of her with his – you know. My, this could be the same party with two people bowing to each other, the red things would be the decorations for the party. Need to get away from them. Never see a man dressed like that, like a Ziegfeld's Folly girl. Nice crown. Nice pelvis, shades of gray show which part further back, looks like textbook illustration. No. No. No. No. No hands, giving a ghostly appearance, but like a costume. No keel, mast, deck-gun sticking out. No shape, it depends on how you dish it out. No special kind. No, the whole body. No, they're standing on their hind legs. No wheels, but that's just sort of cut out. Nope, witches aren't fat like this, this is like toy witches that you punch in school and they fall over and bounce back up at you. Norway here. Nose, eyes and beard of a man. Nose, forehead, cap: just top part of body. Not a good one, distorts time because not the same size on top and on bottom. Not actually red faces but color makes it gay. Not again, I can't look again at that bat, it's too terrible and scary, it's an ugly creature. Not like Merlin's but Santa's elves. Not necessarily blue crabs, seaweed-green. Not physically, like defending his ego. Not such a bad way to die, just suffocated. Not the entire beast. Not this part. Not too clear. Nothing. Nothing. Nothing at all. Nothing, butterflies just look nice. Nothing else. Nothing in particular, you find rats all over. Nothing, just a dead leaf, part of it decaying. Now that's a lotta color, it looks like a couple cats going up a tree in the middle. Now they look like lions. Now this man has hands over his head, sort of like a strong man, muscles bulging. Ocean here, kind you see in geography, usually colored or something else, these gray maps they show in books. Of anyone who might want to hurt them. Of course, it's all dark as an x-ray, it's clearly the inner ear. Of course, the opening in the middle suggests the possibility of escape. Oh, a bat I would say. Oh, a lot of paint. Oh, and a tree, a dead tree. Oh dear, I can't find anything, except maybe two green birds. Oh God, I can't look, I don't know what it is, it's so ugly. Oh God, I don't know, I can't take much more, it's like a plant that can eat you up, it's terrible, don't make me look at it or I'll be crazy more. Oh God, it's that monster chasing me, big black with those huge feet trying to crush me. Oh God, there's two creatures too, they're terrible, they scare me. Oh God, what is it, all the pictures are so scary, just a black ugly bird flying there, so depressing, it's making me sick to see it, take it away. Oh, I don't like this one, it's terrible, like my nightmares. Oh, I know, it's like a frog, I was trying to figure out the bumpiness of it. Oh, I know, it's the little things you see under a microscope, some kind of, a, microorganism, I can't remember the name, oh yes, it's a preemie. Oh, I'd have to – it'd be more accurate to turn it over. Oh, it's magic too, like two genies rising from a magic lamp so to cast a spell on the world. Oh, maybe a butterfly but the coloring is wrong; is that all right?

Oh, maybe a whalechild, yeah, that's right, a whalechild. Oh, my! Oh no, it's got those big branches up here that grab you, I've seen them, they eat people in the parks, see, the green leaves they are deceiving, but the orange leaves can reach out and grab you. Oh no, up here, see the ant, like with wings, like he'll fly up and bite, I can't look it's too awful (*sobs*). Oh, sure, you fill 'em with air and they hold you up, see they come out here, it's for little kids before they know how to swim, I can swim good. Oh, that is probably a mosquito and he's eating on this floor. Oh, that looks like some kind of big thing, like out of science fiction just sort of standing there. Oh, that one's easy, a bat. Oh, that's (*looks at watch*) a monster. Oh that's funny, it's like two people doing their washing or something but they don't look like real people. Oh, that's like girls, like they are dancing or something with their hair up, like ponytail hair, up because they're dancing, or maybe it's not two, just one and she's dancing by the mirror. Oh, that's little girls, like they're playing or fighting. Oh, these green parts look like seahorses, they are really shaped like that. Oh, this looks like the scissors and these would be handles here. Oh, this looks like two dogs, not all of them but just from the middle up and they're playing together, like sniffing at each other the way dogs do that. Oh, this reminds me of a woman, sort of looking herself over in a mirror, she's looking over her shoulder, like to see if everything is all right. Oh, this seems to be two dogs, just this part here (*points*). Oh, very much like this, and they are always red. Oh – what's this?! Oh wow! Oh wow, that looks like a, a, one of those poison things, a scorpion or something, no wait, erase that one. Oh yeah, it looks like the cells are separating, one on each side, like it is spreading out, like when they separate, the main part is in the middle, the white and the red is like the movement of the cell, it's all starting to separate now. Oh yeah, it looks like them pictures of black lungs, like you get if you smoke too much, see, one is here and one is here and they're round like lungs and all black like they are if you smoke too much. Oh yeah, right here (*points*) it looks like a big guy and this part is the sax. Oh yeah, the funny one, it just looks like a woman to me but you can't see her head, and these would be her legs, like the orange part, she's kinda fat and it looks like she's got her legs spread. Oh yeah, this is the penis too. Oh yeah, well I could say that these are hands up here. Oh yes, I remember the blood, well it's up here, the person, see the head, a face is there vaguely, and the arms are down at the sides and the way he's on the post it looks like somebody. Oh yes, it looks milky, not milk, but milky, it's light here and darker here, milky like placenta. Oh yes, right here is the stump and here are his feet, the perspective of this thing makes it look like he's leaning backward. Oh yes, see the dark spots, it looks like if you touch it it would feel bumpy, you know? Oh, you know, it might be like two puppets too, I didn't see it before, here in the dark part, it looks like puppets. Oh, you're really kidding me, aren't you? OK. Oklahoma. Old movies, this is where the gold is. Old washerwomen have always evoked pity in me because I feel sorry they have to work so hard, they're getting older, still have to do that work. Old woman bent over scrubbing. Old-fashioned boots. On either side looks like two reptiles of some sort. On hind legs pointing to diagram of nervous system. On the bottom, two upturned ice cream cones. On the sides are two animals crawling up, like up a tree, like they are trying to reach a branch. On this one? On top, a little animal with pieces missing, head missing, looks like it's sitting down but the head is missing. On top a mountain peak. Once I get a picture in my head it's hard to change. Once when I was painting a house there was a bat stuck behind the shutter, when the bat came out I was scared shit. One here and one here and they're washing clothes in this tub. One seems to be attached to the head of another. One sitting or standing on another's shoulders. One window of a church or building lit with figure far away, indistinct. Only eyes frightened, distrustful like wild eyes. Only outline. Only the center is a clear picture, it's a butterfly, that same red one, he got away. Only the mouth. Only thing I see is an old man with a staff bent over from age. Ooh! Open jaw looks as if it is going to devour something, to come forth with fire. Or a cat. Or as if someone's taken a brain, sort of flattened it (*pushes on table*) all the way back down into the card. Or two people standing, sixty-degree angle to each other, their foreheads are touching, hands are touching. Orange and green is dragon, standing on red, and here is a partition. Orange eye, marks make it look sad. Orange seems to be the chest, vertebrae running down the middle. Orange wings on this back, looking up, a sweep of plumage fans down and back. Organ pipe roughly speaking. Other than that – (*pushes card back*). Outline and color: I think coral reefs are very narrow. Overelongated moth. Pair of butterflies. Pair of dragons insulting each other. Pair of eyeglasses. Pair of hands. Pair of pliers. Pancreas and kidneys. Part of a map perhaps. Part of a totem pole, surmounted by something that looks like a bald eagle. Part of body seen too. Part of intestines; humpy outline here like you see in drawings. Particles of dust. Patty-cake, patty-cake, baker's man. Paved road with two lanes, dark macadam road. Pawn shop, three balls.

Pawnbroker's golden balls. Paws. Paws out like this, fur hanging down, head looks up in air, here the haunches, hind leg haunches. Peace, quiet, no conflict. Pelvic bone. Pelvic bony structure. Penguin or seal, black. Penguin, white belly, feet. Penis. Penis there. People. People. People. People are wearing motorcycle or space-type helmets or armor. People – other people create situations where there's conflict. Perhaps looks more like a water bug. Perhaps the difference in color gave me the feeling of this being more solid and this not. Perhaps they resemble the topographical maps. Pervasive feeling, all animals engaged in aspiration and struggle. Phallic symbol. Photographic view from an airplane. Piece of cloth, to be cut for clothing. Pieces of cellophane held over water. Pink azaleas, clumps of blue, yellow and brown iris around the central pink shrubs. Pink, green, blue, yellow, gold, brown, gray, just about every color I can think of. Pink like a baby. Pink ones almost look like human-type faces, but they have bodies like caterpillars, wearing elfish hats, points going down back, instead of up. Pistachio ice cream. Pleasure and enjoyment. Pointed hats, faces, noses, knees together, hands together, color gives it gay feeling. Pointed orange hats. Possibly a taffeta of two colors, you know the way taffeta comes in related colors. Prehistoric rock. President Eisenhower. Pretty extensive antlers, at each other as if ready to buck. Pretty, let's see. Probably Chinese ink mixed with water. Profiles. Profiles of two unhappy children. Pumpkin. Pushing against leprechauns. Pussycat whiskers. Put on your dress – dress bow – it's the color too! Putting thin glasses up together. Quite fat. Rabbit. Rabbit with ears, wings, attitude of flying. Rams or lambs, cloven hoof, bison, something like that. Rather strange. Real crazy (*laughs*). Really funny, it has big feet, too. Really nothing.

Rear legs of horse. Recently, I've been thinking I see burglars; I'd get my gun and chase them. Red ankle socks. Red 'cause it's going up. Red flames. Red going through here – just colors – gives a feeling of brownishness which is perfectly consistent with the color of bulls. Red might look like snails from the swerve of the thing. Red spots, decorative irrelevance. Red stuff hanging down and on top puts me in mind of a rooster's comb but actually it doesn't look like a rooster. Red things look like seals. Red, yellow and purple butterfly. Reflection in water. Reflection of whole thing in water. Reindeer or dogs. Reminded me of butterfly antennas when I first looked at it. Reminds me of a cigar store Indian; I was on the street once, I looked at a dummy in a window, it looked like a real person. Reminds me of a fantasy: happy playful rabbits. Reminds me of anatomy picture, perhaps of a human body – like physiology classroom – insides open up describing different sections of torso. Reminds me of feelings I had when I was young, when I felt that my parents hated me. Reminds me of me, thinking someday I'll just be able to overcome all the bad feelings I have. Reminds me of my father too, though I hate to keep saying my father. Reminds me of my mother's family. Reminds me of my parents fighting with one another, were actually destroying the family. Reminds me of myself. Reminds me of myself, trying to do myself over, so I'm a prettier person. Reminds me of peasants who came to this country. Reminds me of the color of blood in a blood smear. Reminds me of when I was young, I went to church with my mother. Reminds me of when I was young, my parents took me to StoryLand. Repulsed, but trying to keep control of this – (*points*). Resembles a ship, battleship. Respond is a better word. Rest of gray could be fog, hazy almost like looking at them through water. Rest of orange and red is sides for cars to pass through. Right, a couple of little boys. Right figure looks like a devil, left looks like a king. Right here. Right here. Right here (*points*), it's just the upper parts of the dogs, you can't really see the full body, their noses are touching. Right here (*points*), see they have that big bushiness to them and this is the hill I guess, they have to be way off 'cause they're pretty small. Right here (*points*), they have a lotta legs like crabs. Right here (*points*), they're all colored like African women and they're pulling on this animal here, those people always have a food shortage so when they catch something they pull it apart like this. Right here, looks like tigers or something. Right here, they look exactly like that, I don't suppose you ever took music either but they look just like that with the big handle. Right, it's just a bunch of smoke like rising upward, it's all dark like smoke. Right there, a curved shape. Right through here, the way the outside of it is made. Right up here, it reminds me of the sort of thing you might see in the southwest. Robes, packs, general shape. Rock. Rock formations. Rock masses, feels like rock. Rocks. Roosevelt. Rough drawing of a bomber falling down to earth. Round cheeks, hair up, stone statue, smooth marble. Russian dancers in boots, fur pieces on head, breast, pert noses. Sad creature looking the situation over, like rabbit in *Alice in Wonderland*. Saint Bernards' tongues always hang out. Same thing: female, sex, pleasure. Same things: sex, pleasure, enjoyment. Saw eye, nose and moustache. Saw it moving but it couldn't move sideways except on a work of art. Say, maybe it's that butterfly again. Scaly surface of some kind. Scotties. Scottie's head, ear, snout. Sea urchins. Seafood – can see in restaurants with claws. Seahorse for good luck. Seal climbing down a tree sideways.

Seat. Seaweed or wild plant. Sections of vise that grasps things. See, a couple of eyes in middle of things, eyes of insect in wrong spot. See both sides. See darker colors of walls – main passage and other passage. See head, elbow of crossed arm, and leg. See here, big horns on them, and it's like the legs were up in under, you can't see them well, like they are leaping but I don't know what kind of animal it is. See, here is the rabbit and the white part would be the ice. See – here it is black, then below it's white and to the sides are various grays. See, it's all together up here and these parts are moving up into the full part. See it's here (*points*), it has horns on it, like some weird animal I guess, just the face part. See, like, the top is like this and this is the body (*demonstrates with her body*). See, one on each side and the middle would be the tree, see, it's kind of pointed at the top and has a fuller lower part, they look like cars or something. See, right here. See, symmetrical spots of blood. See the alimentary canal. See, the animals are on the side, like small animals, legs here (*points*) and this is the head and this down here could be a rock and the rest is a tree maybe and they are reaching up for this branch; I suppose it could be anything maybe a bush rather than a tree, but they are reaching up for this part. See, the big wings and the hands and the tail, the crab is inside. See the building, explosion shaded that way, light and dark. See, the different colors of brown there makes it look like some places the fur on him is thick and some is thinner, they're like that, if you ever go to the zoo you see them like this. See the ears and the face and they got these big lips too, and a funny tail out here. See the legs and bodies and heads. See the little head, like it doesn't have much brain in there, and here are the great big feet and the little arms, where the swans are there.

See the little nose and the sort of scrunched-up face, that's the way they look, just here (*points*). See the shape of a giant, it really looks like one and see the size of his feet they is giant too, but he ain't got very big hands, see how little they are, no, wait, not hands, I don't see none but he's got little arms. See the way they are drawn here with all the legs makes them look like that, like spiders. See, the wings are here and it's all red and pink like bloody birds get. See, the wings are here and the body, hey, it really looks a lot like a moth, see (*traces*) it really does, yeah. See, there's one on each side of the stick, they have little antennae like this and it looks like they're really working to lift it up. See these lines, they look hairy to me. See, they have the big hats on like witches wear and big noses but they're not really witches. See this all comes out, like his cheeks and he's got these funny eyes too looking right out, see, right here, like he is mean. See this coloring in here, it gives that impression to me, and it wouldn't be a cat if it wasn't furry. See this right here, with the vertical where the light green extends. Seeing seals jumping around and playing in the park, I like to watch the seals. Seems three-dimensional. Seems to be a prettier butterfly underneath him. Seen from the back, can't see her head, hands up. Separated balls of cotton, soft and fluffy. Set of ears here, folded back. Seven-league boots. Sex, enjoyment, that's all. Sex symbol down here. Sexual intercourse. Sexual intercourse, penis, female organs present, buttocks, anus. Shaded here – looks like stone. Shading here adds to it I suppose. Shading is mold forming on bread mass. Shading is mountain area, lightest parts are flatlands. Shading looks like thick leafy tree, a good shade tree. Shading makes it look fuzzy. Shadows and blotches suggest a not perfectly circular shape, you know the way ice cream cones – it's always misshapen. Shape. Shape and appendages. Shape and head; climbing. Shape, black bear, no real body. Shape, coloring, white and gray stone. Shape inside a heart effect, a real heart. Shape, it has no head, part of tail, more nearly a moth with open wings, color has nothing to do with it. Shape of a pillow. Shape of urn, gray of wrought iron. Shape only. Shape, tail coming out. Shape with pendulum sticking out. Shaped like a heart. Shaped like that. Shaped like two girls, basketball between them, they're bouncing it. Shaped, looks like a rocket, looks like it's going off. Shapes of fallen leaves. Shattered on the bottom. She knows what she thinks, but she doesn't know what she feels. She needs help coordinating the two. She's wearing a dress – I can see the shape of the body under the dress. Shimmery shining light off surface, the effect of light. Short hair. Should I keep the cards like this, or can I turn them around? Should I see more than one? Should I try to find something else? Siamese twins, heads not clear. Sideways it might be a pig, a boar, a wild pig of some kind. Silly person is a goose, I also think of ducks and swans, the story of the ugly duckling, ducks that laughed were the geese, they were silly. Since they're supported against it, it would explain why they can stand up like that with their backs. Sitting on shoulders so legs could come around. Skate fish, or horseshoe crab being washed away, waves. Skate in middle, ocean fish. Skin of a creature that's been nailed up on a wall, like the skin of a raccoon, fur markings and striped fur. Skin of animal on board, furry, striped effect and paws. Sky writing, smoky effect, goes up and down again. Slime. Slowly sifting down, just the shapes of different kinds of leaves, maybe distorted by the wind as they are falling. Sly wolves looking, the dark-light is not unpleasant, like fur.

Small and grayish color. Small dog. Small features, small nose, small paws. Small nose. Smoke. Smoke comes up, women have feathers, smoke looks fluffy. Smoke coming out of nostril and mouth open and big arm is going to slap each other. Smoke looks thick. Smoke spread out, looks like a smudge. Snakes. Snake's head up, ready to come up. Snakes ready to come up. So many different areas marked out by differences in the card, could pick out many creatures; two with gesticulating hands; bird's-crest with body and claw; just separate masses and figures; fantastic creatures; one looks like a bird with animal hindquarters. Soft feelers, eruption underneath the surface. Soft green gelatinous mass. Some big ones sticking out and looks like this (*imitates*). Some bugs have a party. Some bugs have eyes all over, caterpillars have two rows of eyes, these eyes are like that. Some Chinese blood. Some deer. Some green in the middle, looks like the nose of some kind of animal, I can't think of what kind, maybe a pig snout. Some insides or something. Some kind of mythical animal with animal shape and wings. Some oil derricks are further than others. Some old tattered pelt, it looks like it's still got some fur on it from the marks, but not much and it's pretty dirty. Some parts look like it might be part of a map. Some sort of animal there. Some sort of ball, gay, colorful, dancers, all animals: *a*) green caterpillars, *b*) lobsters, *c*) crayfish; just numerous crustaceans – gay. Some sort of decorations, it could be animal's decorations since this center part looks like a butterfly. Some sort of design. Some sort of map. Some sort of sundial in a garden. Some sort of vegetation; partly the color. Someone very mean. Someone who is overwhelmed by circumstances beyond that person's control. Someone's flattened it. Something against their mouths. Something all torn up, like a butterfly I guess. Something almost white about it – ghost face. Something erupting, fire erupting. Something erupting, maybe a penis throwing off sperm, or something with tender feelings is sticking out, tender on top with lot of eruption underneath. Something hanging from the wall. Something like a bull's head. Something like a butterfly. Something like a canal. Something like a valley and the rest are mountains, so rigid and uneven. Something or something's shoulders holding something up. Something that breaks very easily, that's inflexible. Something vaginal about center portion here. Something very sneaky, very isolated. Sometimes I feel I'm still tied to the umbilical cord, I haven't broken ties to my parents I should have by now. Sometimes I see it, sometimes I don't let myself see it. Sort of gulch, mountain ridge heavily wooded, like timber line. Sort of helpless. Sort of horns, open mouths, sort of sitting down like. Sort of like flame of candle but don't see any candle here. Spain, the Bay of Biscay, Gibraltar, the top of Africa and the Suez. Sperm with tail going. Spiders, on the outside. Spinal column dissected and opened up. Spinal cord. Spinal cord dissected, thin line is nervous tissue. Splashes of color like fireworks in the sky, random figures. Split down the center; backbone; mottled like a pelt. Spots on lungs, chest area. Square part here the nose. Squatting hands up, knees, heads, disappear. Stage curtains being pulled apart, center shows lighted stage. Stage curtains would bunch this way. Stage is white from bright lights. Standing, arms out to sides, wide sleeves, large and open. Standing chest to chest, point antlers at each other, as if to buck. Standing on their back left foot, holding on with front legs. Started out as distinct whitish background, leaves on it now. Starting with the gray remains of last year, everything becomes alive again and there is the rosy tint of renewed hope. Starts as the shirt of a man, then here are his arms and going up to his collar. Statue of a native, basket on its head, container takes away from its beauty, supposed to preserve it. Statues of two Greek nymphs. Steam raises the genies. Sticks. Still looks like bear skin except this doesn't belong there. Stories of Peter Rabbit and Uncle Wiggly. Story of a fourteen-year-old boy, he lived in my town, he died sniffing glue. Story of Moses wandering in the wilderness, wandering, looking for the promised land. Stretched out to dry, soft fur of animal drying unevenly. Stretched-out skin of animal, furry texture, lines down back and on legs. String, tongue sticking out already, feet suspended from string, not real human quality. Stump, not really, looks like he's sort of old. Suggestive of a bagpipe, but no pipes. Sunrise, varied colors. Supposed to have a magical quality, put people in a trance. Sure are hard. Sure, I said that before, didn't you listen? Sure, it's here (*points*) and it's got blood on it so it must be a bloody nose like it got hurt. Sure, see the shininess of the color makes it look hard like beetle's. Sure, see up here is the heads and the kinda big body and see the red on the heads and down here would be the blood, it's pretty messy. Sure, you can only see their noses like they're ready to chomp on you. Swirl effect, laminated. Sylvester, that's his name, he's a kinda dumb cat and he's always getting run over because he's after a little bird that always gets away. Symbol of airman's death. Symmetry is so it could be a butterfly. Tail, head; I saw pictures – this could be dinosaur too – but this part is realistic. Teeth. Tell me again what I'm supposed to do. That black part ain't nothin', but the white looks like a stingray, like you might see at the beach. That could be a rabbit in the center. That is its leg. That looks like a bat if you don't use the outer parts. That looks like a flying cat, is what it looks like, with a horse's mouth, 'cause it has a long mouth, looks like it has a big bottom too. That looks like a rocketship taking off from a platform with fireworks that are holding cotton candy. That looks like an old blanket, some of the fur has worn off. That looks like two Indians sitting together, they have things on their heads. That looks like two witches sitting in green chairs with pink rocks under them. That looks like walking beavers, they're going to climb up a tree, bouncing on the hill, they're trying to get the leaves. That one looks like a butterfly or a bat, but looks more like a bat. That one looks real hard! That reminds me of a squashed cat. That reminds me of that moth again, the one I saw before flying along with its wings out. That sex symbol again; it's crazy. That thing looks like a monster with a pogo stick. That's a bearskin rug with a piece attached to it that has nothing to do with it. That's a big horse, he's running this direction. That's a butterflower. That's a skeleton and he's got blood on his hands, I don't want to do this anymore. That's a spider that caught a goat. That's about all. That's all. That's all. That's all. That's all. That's all. That's all furry, it's like a cat, like on TV, I can't remember his name but he's always getting run over by something and he gets flat like this, do you know which one I mean? That's all I see. That's all I see on that one. That's all they have left, they were wiped out at the Little Bighorn. That's it. That's it. That's it. That's its feet. That's like a butterfly, a pretty one. That's like a flower before it opens up. That's like a monster that you might see in a comic book. That's like a voodoo doll up there on the top. That's like one of those badges that a forest ranger wears. That's like two teddy bears kissing.

That's not too good is it, well I was thinking like at night, it's all dark like that and the different shadows give it a rounded effect, like billowy and it's all like moving upward (*motions with hands*). That's really all I can find. That's so ugly, why would a butterfly which is so beautiful land on this ugly part? That's strange, I know, but it's what it looks like. That's the first thing that came to mind, but I don't know. That's the way they should be on a butterfly. That's what it looks like. That's what they are sitting on. That's when I get angry, when there's a conflict inside of me. The A-bomb cloud. The blue is water, anybody knows that. The blue might be flags. The blue parts could be two flags too. The body is narrow and the width gave me the feeling of a ruff. The buildings are so small, they must be way off in the distance, and they look like on this mountain, see this part here would be the mountain, see the peaks of the buildings are here (*points and outlines with her fingernail*). The center could be a ditch. The center could be a vase, the white area here. The center is a well-traveled path. The center of the explosion is always calm, but the rest is full of action. The center part could be a crab. The center part looks like a vase. The center white part makes me think of a keyhole. The central structure – whatever that is. The clumsiness. The color. The color and the shape. The color is sort of shaded in some way. The color makes it look like that. The color of terriers and the faces are shaped like some I've seen. The coloring of it. The coloring too is blustery, how the wind is represented. The colors of springtime and rebirth. The colors show the different countries, these are the waterways. The colors there, they look like fur on his back and here is his nose and head and his legs, like he got flattened out, ouch! The comb effect here. The dark central column is one, the light gray shade makes the bell-bottom pants, high-heel type boots with small toe, sort of disappears here. The dark part represents the shadow effect and when you draw you sometimes don't use all the lines, like you use the shadow effect to create an impression. The dark spots look like two elephants, facing each other, heads raised, trunks in air, front feet up, like standing together. The darker spot could be an eye set in the middle of the skull. The delicacy of an etching. The design, though, from a purely abstract angle, is rather interesting, just from the point of view of balance and composition. The devil was always a figure that I feared, it entered into my episode in January, I felt I was somehow in confrontation with the devil. The different coloring makes it look like that, like the handle is darker than the churn. The different colors, the shades it has, I got a headache. The different shades look like the different colors. The difficulty of living twenty-four hours a day, you never have it made, it's always a struggle. The dog got kicked around the house too, but the cat didn't get hurt too bad. The eyes have a mild expression just like the cow I saw yesterday. The face is in here, outlined by the white. The faces are very angular, short haircut, not a very human appearance, but the nose gives a very proper appearance. The feet. The first thing I think of here is the emblem used by one of the motion picture companies in introducing their films. The goddess is in the center and there is the darkness on each side as if it might be smoke or fog, it sort of illustrates the mysteries about the gods and goddesses. The gray. The gray color of the rocks and the shading. The grays vary here and get so intense they are almost black. The hands of that person (*points to middle*). The head is looking back up, neck's curved around like that. The heads, and arms here, and body. The helmet sits down low, gray goes over eyes, maybe as blinders as if camel was to be used in war. The hoof here. The inside of a heart. The jackets, or whatever, have lapels or collars, stuffed-shirt sort of appearance, why I thought of tuxedos. The kind of puppets I'm thinking of have heads bigger than the body parts, like this. The large area would be the umbrella part and this would be the handle, it's really more like a beach umbrella than one you carry because the top is so big in relation to the handle. The lungs of a chicken down in here like when you dissect a chicken. The man could have wings, more of a man than a woman, sort of a superman with wings. The map of Italy showing mountains and valley. The mask, or whatever, is not shaped like anything, looks more demoniacal, not human, takes away from its monk appearance. The men are over-civilized, birdlike, too refined, too effeminate. The men look like homosexuals. The middle red part reminds me of a bright red bow I used to wear in my hair when I went to Sunday school. The mouth is not distinct. The natural course of events. The one on top is wearing boots. The open mouths and the expression. The outer figures look like two knights extending their – The part around the straight line here. The part here. The part here and it looks like it was coming out of a cloud. The picture as a whole an appearance of a deer, with eyes and nostrils, with a red mark upon its nose. The pictures I've seen are usually very colorful like this, I think they call them buttes or something, it has that sort of shape to it. The pink coming out of orange, conquered green and gray with paw. The pink looks like an animal if you turn it this way, like a cat or something. The pink looks like some apples, I think four of them but two are back behind the front two, I'm getting hungry, and these look nice and red like ready to eat. The pink's about the color of blood in a blood smear. The plan or blueprint of cave with passages. The purple is the face, pink hats, cloth-kind falling back. The rabbit is clear. The red colors made me think of lobsters, long feelers, sea grass is green with holes in it. The red in middle looks like a brassiere. The red splotch. The red thing looks like a butterfly on the bottom. The rest of it could be a bat like the other one, see the wings are out like it is maybe flying round. The rest of the card leaves me blank. The robe flows down, doesn't close in the middle, the sleeves hang down. The rough edges around it and the points here. The sea. The shaded part here. The shading in the pink looks like bubbles. The shape. The shape and the tentacles. The shape is like a mountain and the grayness is like a snowcap seen from a great distance. The shape looks like it. The shape, not in motion. The shape of it. The shape of the cloud of the A-bomb. The shape of the face is not human and suggests a strange structure or hair here. The shape of the orange suggests that it's cut off, like a circle-type nose, pig snout. The spots where the eyes should be. The stamen, sepal, petals. The stem looks like a tree and shaped like a tree. The stiffness. The story of Passover, angel of death flying over. The stupidest thing they ever did was to get married. The sun. The tail back here. The thing stuck out right there (*points*). The top of the core is lighter (*points to lighter pink on card*). The top of this pink kind of reminds me of a caterpillar's head, I used to have a collection of them when I was a kid. The top ones have little tails, like shrimp. The top part looks like a totem pole. The top part looks like it could be an Indian totem pole with the carved feathers coming out from each side. The top seems to lighten and give it focus. The top, some type of witch, ghost.

The torso of the body. The totem pole is this dark, decorations at the top. The triangle shape, coming down, to make the eyes slope out. The triangular indentation is suggestive of a front of motorcycle helmet or cavalier's. The two red splashes, looks like lightning flashes illuminating the sky. The upper part, not the pink, but just the upper part reminds me of a picture of an explosion, to represent everything moving outward with all the colors symbolizing the violence of the explosion. The way I felt in relation to my father when I was younger. The way it's made. The way their heads look. The way they are in the body. The white center is the plane, quite like one and all of the darker part is the storm, like clouds of a storm, dark and storm-like, yes, a weather plane, no doubt. The white space gives me the feeling of wide open spaces, freedom. The whole area. The whole blot looks like a symbol for demoniacal flight (*held for a while and turned*). The whole thing. The whole thing looks like an insect. The woman is in the middle, her arms are extended upward, here, and the rest would represent the light radiating outward. The woolly outline. Their heads are thrown back and they're spinning around on one leg. Their stance gives the impression that they're tugging at it, upset at each other. Their whole way of life is gone. Them look like two pinchers that they have and that looks like the tongue right here and them look like antennae. Then it gets darker. Then there is a space of trial and tribulation leading to a mellower period, then life becomes grayer. There are a lot of bright colors here, red, blue, pink and orange. There are the two eyes and dot for the nose. There are tweezers there too, like eyebrow tweezers. There are two bears supporting a corset or pulling it apart. There are two bulls. There are two girls made up to look like bunnies

– if you take heads alone. There are two William Cotton heads, his color as in the green. There are various shades of gray, black and white placed to make a pleasing pattern. There is a feeling of great strength. There is a path, dense woods and suggestions of side roads. There is always something of joy on either side and even the end has a rosy tint. There is another face down here, with horns too. There was a big witch's pot outside, bones inside supposed to be bones of children. There's a butterfly in here too. There's a dead bird there too, he got smashed and is all blood. There's a nose there too that got hurt, it's a bloody nose. There's no top to it. There's one on each side with the legs extended, really pushing against each other (*points*). There's something vulgar about this, it looks like the same thing as before but a different picture of it. There's the eyes. There's two alligators there, and they're peeking out from behind a big bush or something waiting to catch something, wow, I wouldn't want to be around there. There's two dogs too, one here and one here. There's two funny-looking ants too, they're trying to carry that stick there. There's two men here and they are fighting. These are black and white. These are bloodstains, ugly, do I have to look at it? These are bulls with golden horns, it is symbolic, in flight. These are just colors, red, blue, green, brown. These are just fossils. These are kinda funny, aren't they, like I suppose it could be a bat if you think about it. These are like telegraph signals. These are lots of grays. These are mouths, forehead, hair, chin, mouths. These are orange ones with the big pointed hat, we got one something like it for our daughter. These are ridiculous cards, did you make them? These are so weird it's hard to make anything of them. These are spinning around the center. These are such intense shades of gray. These are the bushes, you get the impression that they are back up on a small hill, you see all of this, this would be the hill, maybe they're small trees and the white and black parts here are the hill, you have to look in perspective to see it; do you understand? These are the crabs and the wishbones, this would be antennae and claws and the round body, so they are like crabs. These are the eyes, they make it look unfriendly. These are the handles and you pull 'em apart and this thing in the center contains a spring-like thing and it pulls against you and you do that a lot every day to build up your muscles. These are the noses and the heads and these are their necks. These are the rays shooting out of them, like the sun, it has rays (*demonstrates the sun's rays using her body*). These are the wings and the little body and you can see the streak of colors in it, like there would be on a real butterfly, like if the colors that are supposed to be were really there. These are two arms, hands reaching toward each other. These are two heads facing each other, talking. These are two rabbits that are kissing together, like they're in love. These blue networks of lines. These brown things look like deer like they are jumping over something, you see horns and they're brown. These brown things look like two buffaloes, brown and shaggy. These clouds look like they might be people. These could be spiders, I don't like spiders, these are blue spiders though and they don't harm things. These got all these legs and these have antennae and stuff and these got the head and body shaped like an ant. These green things could be those animals with a horn in their head, like they used to have a long time ago. These images remind me of him, especially because they're white. These little green parts could be grasshoppers. These look a little like arms. These look like bears and this looks like a tree. These look like dinosaurs. These look like horns up here and these look like the face part and this looks like the mouth. These look like legs out here one on each side. These look like spiders and these look like termites, these look like ants and these look like lights and this looks like all the food here. These look like the heads of two swans, they are supposed to be white but these are black. These look like whiskers. These marks are strata, a stream or river. These might be a pair of very, very plump roosters, with plump little bosoms, facing each other. These other blue things look like crabs. These outer red parts look like two candy apples. These parts here look like cups, like coffee cups or beer mugs with the handle here. These red top parts could be two gnomes, there is the impression that they are arguing with each other. These slits here could be eyes too, like from a science fiction monster or something. These things could be dogs, one on each side. These things could be fishhooks too, there's no line though. These things here look like crabs and they're fighting over this weed thing in between them. These things in middle look like cannons firing across ocean, anti-aircraft guns. These things kinda look like a couple of big collie dogs. These two animals that got stuck on a tree. These two look like feet, here, head or tail of an animal. These two might be pink dwarfs – no, babies facing each other. These would be the wings and here are the antennae like they use like radar to find their way and the rest is just the body part. These yellow things look like somebody dropped some eggs and they broke all over, I did that once and was my mom mad, see the yolk is running into the other part like if you break them, the yolk breaks too sometimes and it makes the whole thing yellow like this. They all blend and fuse in the center but spread out and are thinned with the white. They all look like they have that sex symbol, a uterus, I don't understand it. They are a different kind of spider 'cause they can even stand up on their legs like this and they're eating this thing, maybe a stick. They are almost rearing away from the central object but their eyes remain looking at it, half bowing as though they know they should be polite but each wants the seat. They are apt to be a woman's rather than a man's because they are slender and the sleeves are rather tight-fitting. They are butting heads right now as they do in those fierce death struggles that they have, see the horns and the legs are extended with the muscles almost bulging through the skin. They are picking at something but not a crab, but you can see it like a crab too. They are precisely like this, I should have thought of it first, I'm sure the staples are there in the middle. They are pretty, life should be like that, see how pretty the yellow is and they are beautiful. They are tiny so they must be eyebrow tweezers, other tweezers are bigger, see this tiny part here, it does look like that. They are usually brown like this and they are shaped like an upside-down V with the pods on the end like these, see here (*points*). They are very graceful. They aren't real animals, at least not now, but the Greeks used to have them, I don't know the name but I know we studied them, you know what I'm talking about. They bite indiscriminately, anybody, might bite me. They could stand on the very tips. They don't look like much, I can't be sure but maybe it's two people facing each other like they're standing up there and they have their hands down at their sides. They don't seem to be passive and the front paws seem to be pushing. They fix their hair like that. They fried them, but they're not round because they're forming them and they don't come out like the ones you buy, see, like just this black part and of course there's the hole. They got four legs. They got red faces and that looks like a beak. They have a definite front, separate from the darkness behind, but the back sort of looks like you're looking through water or a fog. They have a lot of legs, just like crabs, I suppose this is what they look like, they're not blue though, not real crabs. They have a shape of deer sort of jumping, see the horns and the legs, just deer. They have all those legs, here the blue, see, they are ugly like spiders, yuck. They have big ears and the short snout, it's just the faces, you can see the eye in the one, see here (*points*). They have feathers sticking up in their hair that's why I thought they'd be playing Indian, they're just like laughing at each other. They have lots of legs like this, they could be spiders but spiders aren't blue, I'm sure of that. They have one leg and one is obscured. They have ponytails sticking out, reminds me of pictures of people in the fifties with ponytails. They have so many legs, creepy and crawly things but there they are two of them, and they aren't so bad because they are the blue variety or species which makes them friendly. They hurt my dog one time. They just come out here, one on each side, the tree isn't there, but just this part (*points*), it's like roots, see the little finger like ends, like roots. They just have that shape to them and buffaloes are brown like this and they look shaggy. They just look all yellow the way broken eggs look, see them, the darker part in there is what's left of the yolk, like it's running into the white part. They just remind me of that, they have that shape to them, see on either side, just tree roots. They just seemed to remind me of that, the way they are formed there and the handle out here. They look all funny, scrawny like they didn't eat much, maybe they're clowns 'cause you see clowns doing something like that to be funny. They look blind. They look like smoke, like the clouds but they have faces and body parts and here is the magic lamp, it's spooky but I like it 'cause I understand magic. They look like they are not trying very hard to hide their hands. They might be shaking hands or something, it could be a costume party because they are wearing big red hats, probably two women who are greeting each other; see these are the hats and this would be the rest of them, as if they have long dresses on. They said to me, 'The witch can get you', or something like that (*laughs*). They scared the hell out of me. They seem about to fall. They seem insignificant and helpless; again, like victims. They seem to be clapping hands. They seem to be straining over this in the middle as if they are trying to lift it but it may be too heavy, see the heads and arms out here and the legs. They seem very – don't seem very solid to me – seem very shallow, very tenuous. They – they're kinda shaped like beavers and a flat tail right here. They usually lay out the flowers like in a design on the grave, you know everybody sends flowers and they have to do something with them, and they try to get the colors to match, sort of like this, see the colors are the same on each side, like a design, it's like that. They were on opposite sides of the card. They would have incense in the church. They'd always be fighting with the cat. They'd be standing guard outside the temple. They'd belong only in a circus. They'd have an awful hard time, because it's slanting back. They're awful, I don't like them. They're blind, they can't see what they're doing. They're distorted to a certain extent, legs seem a bit longer than would be proper. They're finishing off a decaying body left in the weeds. They're getting ready to cook somebody. They're girls, they have ponytails sticking up, out in the air. They're like boxing at each other, see each one has his arms out like they are hitting each other. They're like you make in the fall, at least I do for the kids, they look like they've been dipped in the red candy syrup, when you do this they take on this color, see, just these round parts here (*points*). They're pointed. They're sort of at an angle, not completely upturned. They're sort of wearing spacesuits. They're trying to decide who is the wickedest 'cause they're pointing their fingers at each other. They're very small, here and here, with little peaks on their heads, and they're green, I don't know what kind they might be, just birds. They're very unrealistic about eating worms, you can see they'll never be able to do it. They're watching each other to see what they can get out of each other. They're white like lights on, if they weren't on it would all be black, this is the little chimney. Thick form, no tail. Thick smoke, sort of in a spiral, might have been a heavy oil fire. Things playing on little bagpipes. This a man's head, here too. This again – kind of a cross-section of human when you take skin off and have muscles on each side and muscles above stomach, stomach is the pink, ribs and on into the neck of the person. This all looks like a floral design with the different flowers arranged so that one is on each side, it's very pretty. This bell shape down here. This bottom is like when the sun hits the water, it looks like that. This bottom part kinda looks like a statue of a couple of frog heads, like maybe in a museum. This butterfly has these colors. This card is especially sexual, I think. This center blue looks like part of a bone structure, not the whole bone, what do you call it, the sternum I think, this is like half of it. This center blue might be a bat like here's one wing and the other and I really don't see anything else. This center looks like something too, a beetle I think, or some kind of bug, it's all black, ugly, I like the angel better, this has a hard shell, you can tell. This center part could be a canal too, like down in a ditch. This center part looks like a hole in the ground to me, you can see the folds of the edge around it like it was just going down like a well. This central portion, women with huge pompadours; they are peculiar. This color looks like skin to me, the part being cut is lighter colors and this object is the penis. This could be a couple of crabs. This could be a maple seed like it's falling off a tree and spinning down. This could be a maple seed, with the little pods on the end. This could be a mouth. This could be another couple of crabs, here in these blue parts. This could be the steeple, here the door, I don't know why, it looks like a church to me. This could be tree roots I guess, the way they come out on the sides, there's one on each side, just roots. This could be two children, one here and one here, just from the waist up. This could be two dogs standing on their front legs, no, I mean their back legs, pushing with the front ones. This dark spot could be an eye. This don't look like nothin' but smoke. This green-blue grass is pretty, picture of mountains far off, color is like Adirondacks. This is a bear skin rug. This is a difficult one, but if I look this way I can see a chair, sort of a Victorian chair. This is a hard one but I guess it could be a butterfly if you don't have to include these things out here. This is a little fish, the little pink thing. This is a watercolor exercise perhaps. This is a woman standing with hands raised and feet together. This is an idiot child with tongue hanging out. This is another weird one, that looks like a red butterfly there but I don't think I ever saw a red butterfly, maybe it's an African one, they got a lot of weird things there. This is blood all over here and the skeleton is right inside, like this dark part, that's where skeletons always are. This is creation. This is hard! This is Hell and Heaven on top and here are the forces keeping them apart. This is how a woman looks if she inspects herself in the mirror for cancer, these are really awful pictures (*giggles*). This is its body. This is light gray. This is like a cartoon cat that just got run over with a steam-roller. This is like water wings that you use when you learn to swim, can you swim? This is one of those white globes used in a kitchen. This is rock. This is something I'd like to have on the floor and be able to step on. This is the back and they are standing on hind legs and pushing forward with front legs. This is the handle. This is the spine and the ribs, see right here, you can see it's shaped like that is shaped. This is the top and it gets wider toward the bottom and here is the trunk, like a triangle effect, like pine trees have that, you know? This is the trunk and the rest is all the branches and leaves, just all spread out like a big tree. This is the typical pose. This is weird, it looks like the body of a woman, she's got no head but she's like laying there with her legs apart. This just like a lotta paint that somebody threw and it landed that way. This king reminds me of the little king in the pictures the other day. This larger part only, not the top part but just this bigger section, it reminds me of a piece of fur. This lighter bluish spot. This looks like a better bat. This looks like a big umbrella tree. This looks like a bird, vaguely of course, it's really just a cloud. This looks like a brass post. This looks like a couple of animals climbing a tree or something. This looks like a couple of those toy clowns like kids bat around. This looks like a cross-section of a lake been drained dry. This looks like a doll's head or dummy's head, something made of papier maché, very stylized, back to back. This looks like a horse's head with angry expression in eyes but body form incongruous. This looks like a mountain here and two bears on each side. This looks like a nipple up here. This looks like a pelt to me, like the skin off of some furry animal. This looks like a piece of tissue paper because of the way the light seems to come through it. This looks like a very bad case of tuberculosis shown in x-ray. This looks like a woman's leg kicking out. This looks like a wooden totem pole that the Indians have, with faces on them. This looks like his head and arms and big old feet, and I didn't use this part. This looks like ponytails, this looks like the outline of the face and this looks like the back part of them, and it looks like they are laughing at each other. This looks like smoke down here. This looks like some hideous science-fiction monster, as if he's sitting on like a big tail, maybe he's thinking. This looks like some kind of animal with big horns, see two of them, like they were leaping forward. This looks like some kind of monster or something, there's really big feet and a face up here, like the face of a bird or something. This looks like something from a biology book, an illustration of internal parts like the lungs and rib cage and maybe the stomach, I'm not sure of the parts but it does look like those illustrations. This looks like something that got split apart, like a rabbit I guess. This looks like the bronchial tube and lungs. This looks like the face, and this looks like the body and the hands. This looks like the Fisk Tire ad. This looks like the horns and this looks like where they cut it, it is jagged. This looks like the lava coming down and this looks like the volcano. This looks like the outline around the heart and this looks like the heart. This looks like the tables they are sitting at. This looks like the trunk, and center looks like the covering on the tree, like leaves. This looks like two deer in a death struggle, I don't really care for it. This looks like two statues, like of people who are looking at each other; it's kinda funny, you know? This looks like two women holding a bowl, trying to lift a big bowl. This looks like where the king's throne is up here and these look like two people fanning him. This looks like where they look out, two eyes. This looks near; this looks far away. This lower part could be ice cream or maybe sherbet, yes, like orange and raspberry sherbet. This lower part reminds me of exposed flesh, as if it might be a burn or something like that. This might be a butterfly. This might be a piece of sea foam washed up on the beach. This might be two little dogs playing together, they're rubbing their noses together. This one isn't a collie though, it's just like some other kind, just laying there, see the head and the body, like the feet were curled up in under like dogs lay, like that. This one isn't the same, it's more like a rug might be instead of a trophy skin, it has more fur (*rubs blot*), see the lines all over and these extensions are the legs. This one looks furry too, see the shades give that effect and it has the four legs, or what were legs, yes, like a rug I'd say. This one looks like it's trying to get this paw up to pull itself on to the upper story. This one's all mixed up, the blue things could be spiders but spiders aren't blue. This other part doesn't look like it would go with it though. This other part looks like a bearskin of some kind. This part could be a fish too. This part here could be a shellfish of some sort, we study them in science, they have the funny shell with the crease in it. This part is like two weird people trying to hurt each other with this big stick-like thing. This part looks like a weird-looking person kind of like staring at you, ugh, that's all. This part looks like people here, see just the top part of the pink. This part reminds me of a man playing a saxophone. This part reminds me of ribs or something like some insides. This part shaped like – the colors and stuff. This person's head extends into a mask, collar of robe. This pink and orange will be a lady's blouse. This pink could be a bloodstain. This pink is like a cloud that is all fluffy and colored because the sun is hitting it. This pink is like bubble gum. This pink, red, you know, it's like sea coral that you see skin diving, it's kinda long like this and it's red, that means it can be poison if you get cut on it. This really doesn't look like that but the overall shape of the thing can be interpreted that way. This red part is the ears, although they're not supposed to be red and here is the head and the body part and little feet. This red part looks like something all exploding, like a bomb. This reminds me of something from a biology book, illustrating the insides, everything is in pairs, almost everything. This resembles two figures in argument, or a modern dance form, arms outstretched. This right here (*points*). This stuff reminds me of pictures of Grand Canyon, colored pictures with canyon going down. This thing looks like a fly. This top looks like a gray lizard, ugh! This top part looks like an insect, maybe like a fly. This top portion looks like Fujiyama, distinct peak. This up here shaped like a tree – the top of a pine tree – and these look like branches. This way I see another dog, like laying down here, see here (*points*). This way it looks like a bear crossing a pond and he's seeing himself in the water. This way it looks like a dog standing on some rocks or things. This way it looks like a spooky house. This way it looks like two women dancing, like dancing the cancan or something. This way like fruit: four beets, two cabbages, two carrots. This way the green part looks like a fat guy playing a saxophone.

This way they look like birds, they're hiding. This way you can see another person's side view again, like on the last one. This white part in here looks like something, like a waterfall maybe with the kind of blue around it like a waterfall has, see it's this white part (*points*) and it has some blue and then out here it's like green like around a waterfall. This white part looks like a bird, see the wings way out like (*points*). This whole center section reminds me of some sort of organ, like the tubes in the stomach or somewhere, as if it is open like it was dissected. This would be her head and her arm and legs, looking over her shoulder in the mirror and here's her reflection, maybe she's checking to see if her skirt is straight or something, women do that a lot, I suppose. This would be the feet and that's the arm and this would be the enormous body, I discounted this piece when I looked at it. This would be the handle and the churn part and it's kinda colored that way too. This would be two people, men I think and they're struggling to lift something up. This would suggest it because of narrow opening and this would also be the womb, the color makes it look like diagrams in a book. This wrinkled part looks like overalls. This, yeah, it's like a butterfly, this reminds me of a whole body and these are the wings and the wings are out this way like a butterfly has wings out this way. Those are the feathers. Those look like soft pillows in a feminine house, like in bedroom of Louis XV. Those outer parts sort of look like tree roots. Those people, they give the appearance of arguing, fighting over the head. Three balls of pawnbroker. Three pairs of funny-looking birds: gray set, green set, yellow set. Tie is lopsided. Tinge of yellow, greenish-blue tinge, there's nose and eye and shock of hair. To me it looks like a person on a post with his arms out and legs down, and down here is a lot of blood like they shot him. Tongue hanging out. Tongues hanging out, nose to nose. Too vague to me so I can't describe it. Tooth in center. Top looks like a negative of a photograph of a brightly colored butterfly. Top part looks like a bird sitting on something. Torn pieces of material, silk, the color and form, couldn't be velvet because not heavy enough texture. Totem pole looks carved because of the shading. Tree, tints of yellow, these leaves about to fall off because they are different colors, not green, you can see the way it looks in the water here. Tropical climates and, just a wish I used to have, to live on a tropical island by myself, but not anymore I don't like to be by myself anymore. Truncated eagle-like creature holding a crab-like one; like on a coat of arms. Trunk of tree looks rough. Tube, wind bag, shape. Turtle with lots of heads. Two acorns. Two African dancers. Two angels. Two angry octopus-men looking mad. Two apes on fire. Two badgers trying to climb up to the top of something. Two bears dancing. Two bears toasting each other, mugs raised. Two beavers climbing a tree, I don't know if they climb trees or not, but it doesn't matter, does it? Two beetles arguing with one another. Two big spiders coming at them from the outside. Two birds dressed up, looks like carrying a basket. Two blue crabs eating green seaweed. Two boys crawling up a pole on top. Two boys or young tough men with pug noses, wild green hair, probably Irish. Two bulls. Two cannibals over a brewing pot. Two chickens with their hands pushing away from each other. Two crabs and coral. Two crabs on either side. Two crickets sassing each other. Two crocodiles, looks like they're about to die. Two dancing ladies, each is missing a leg, an arm and a head. Two devils. Two dogs. Two dogs rubbing noses. Two dogs, setters, with sort of French poodle-like trimmings. Two ears back of rabbit's head. Two eyes, cheeks; these fit around the ears. Two faces in the middle, on either side. Two figures wearing parasols, promenading, swaying, carrying kerchiefs like mid-Victorian, maybe they are posing, because of unnatural stance, long gowns with ruffling up the back. Two frogs engaged in a rather profound discussion on the structure of the nervous system of which they have diagram right behind them. Two genies coming out of a bottle, facing each other. Two girls folk-dancing with their hands up in the air. Two girls playing basketball. Two gold things, statues of a lion. Two groundhogs walking up a mountain. Two horses. Two kangaroos pulling at something. Two Kenyan dancers, they fix their hair like that, in an upward motion, and these look like dresses and stuff. Two ladies in turbans playing cards. Two lambs without front feet. Two lambs, young ones spring up. Two little bats without wings. Two little boys looking very nasty. Two little girls having an argument, each pointing in a different direction, I think maybe they're Indians wearing feathers; I don't see anything else. Two little puppets on strings. Two little rabbits who just jumped on rocks. Two little Santa Claus-like men carrying packs. Two little woodpeckers trying to eat two big green worms. Two men dancing a Spanish dance. Two men in fluffy, shiny Spanish costume, it looks like a Spanish dance because of the way they look. Two men in full dress, in conflict over organs of woman which are swinging, hanging, hitting men in head. Two men in tail coats, white collars bending over a table. Two men sleep-ing on hillside peacefully snoring. Two men squatting doing a folk dance, sort of a Russian dance. Two men trying to lift a cauldron. Two men with beards, white celluloid collars and dress suits. Two middle-aged men with big noses.

Two monkeys, warming their hands over a fire. Two Negro boys kicking their feet away, very ludicrous, nothing to do with reality. Two newborn babies. Two nuns with white surplice, heads here, and black garb. Two of 'em, see the yellow it's like, whatdaucallem little yellow flowers but not opened yet, see here. Two old colored men with backs toward each other with hands up in air. Two old ladies in rocking chairs, blankets on laps, knee to knee, and long hair, mainly in ponytails, sticking straight up, like they're falling. Two old men sleeping. Two old washerwomen working very hard. Two people falling through the air. Two people, maybe dressed up in tuxedos, fancy people, maybe waiters. Two people with a funny hat on and they have guns just like they're shooting at each other. Two pink creatures, with heads facing away from each other, human. Two profiles of Alfred Hitchcock. Two rats at each side, they're going up to the top of something. Two rocks precariously balanced on a ledge. Two sides and in middle a cocoon, butterflies coming out of cocoon. Two small lambs looking up at him. Two stout Turks doing a ritual dance. Two support chambers connected by white spots. Two surprised and embarrassed young men, both have discovered that they have tickets for the same seat. Two things sticking up in air, shape, color. Two witches again. Two witches in dark part. Two witches over a brewing pot. Two witches smoking cigars. Two women facing, agitated attitudes, the lines shooting; profiles: thrust chin, prominent, glaring. Two women, fighting, only their heads. Two women pulling apart a purse, that's it. Two women with sassy expressions. Two women's half-breasts. Type of shading reminiscent of Will Cotton's drawings. Ubangi lips. Ugh, more spiders, up here there's two, see the blue ones. Ugh, this looks like some sort of big monster, all covered with fur, like from science fiction, some huge thing just standing there, it looks like he has big boots on. Uh, hmm. Uh, hmm, I don't know. Uh huh. Uh huh. Uh huh. Uh huh, and it has wings. Underneath green looks like a pretty good Saint Bernard, but they'd have to be wearing chef's hats on their heads to account for the whole green shape. Underneath them are two younger men who're sleeping. Unless it's wood or something that they can get their claws into. Up further the skull of a cow, or deer, horns, nostrils at bottom, two sets of nostrils really. Up here. Up here, if I turn it this way it looks like two little ants are trying to lift a big stick or something, like here see it (*points*) here they are. Up here it looks like a sunrise, with the rays of the sun just showing from behind this thing, maybe a tree. Up here it looks like two girls looking at each other, they each have a ponytail. Up here, the orange part, see the pointy hats and these would be the guns and the faces and fat bodies and the way it's here you can see the bullets going back and forth, see these lines here, these would be the bullets from the guns. Upturned nose, looks impish. Urn, old-fashioned, iron arms. Vaginal opening with surrounding dark area, looks like soft hair. Vertebrae column like an x-ray picture. Very dissatisfied with their lives. Very happy and joyful, uninhibited women. Very old and – once, my mother had to put stuff in my eyes, I couldn't see. Very pointed ears. Very quickly and without warning. Victims. Viola, with something on the wood, like cello. Vise holds tools, holds things together. Waiters in uniform pulling a table. Wall is all black part. Walt Disney. Wanting to refuse to do something but knowing I have to do it. Wants to devour the other one, because it isn't pretty. Was going to say a moth again, but was bored with moths.

Water. Waterfall coming over the mountain. Way it's made, the shape of it. Way it's shaped. Way standing up, looks like they are up on their legs. We always had rats in the house when I was a kid. We have a tapestry at home has Chinese dragon, here face and eye, and it is blue. We used to pick wishbones, my mother would say, 'Make a wish.' Weird-looking, as though leering. Well, a vase, like you have to look at it like I am, I've done some drawing and this has the forms and the shadows like you might use if you draw a vase. Well, all of it, this would be wings and here is the tail and the antennae. Well, ants are very hard workers and they're lifting this stick like they are cooperating, like you see on *Sesame Street*, see the little feelers there and their tiny legs? Well anyhow, they are like women, and they are probably carrying this basket here. Well, everybody knows clouds are white but sometimes when the sun hits like this they get colored, this one is pink like maybe the sun would be behind it or something, just pink, and see the lines in there, they make it look fluffy, like some clouds are. Well, he has black eyes, here, and this is the nostrils, see they're red or pink, and these are the ears, see the other red things, and out here are the cheeks, they're fat-looking like a cat's face. Well, here and here, like little birds and they're under this bush, see the green is the bush and they're like oriole birds 'cause they're orange like oriole birds and they're under, see, where the bush covers part of them right here like they are hiding. Well, here are the eyes and the nostrils and the shaggy chin and he has a white forehead, his eyes are slanted sort of and so he must be mad. Well, here is the head (*points*) and the legs are out here on the side, it just looks like a frog. Well, he's all black, like a big gorilla with these big boots here (*points*) and these are his arms and his head is kinda pulled in like he's lookin' for something, or maybe expectin' a fight, mean-lookin'. Well, he's got his legs out here and here and he's got his head down like he was coming right at me, like when they race they put their head down. Well, he's got his wings out like he was flying, and his little body and his hands out in the front, we saw them in a movie in school, just like this I think. Well, he's on this post, just sitting there like waiting for something to swim by so he can grab it, just trying to look like he's not there, see he's just there (*runs finger around blot*) on this (*points*) post. Well, he's probably eating the milk spots. Well, he's sure got a long tail draggin' there, and little arms and big monster feet like he's just lumbering along nice and easy. Well, I can see two people facing each other, a pole in back. Well, I can't really identify any of the flowers, they don't really look like any that I am familiar with but they are very pretty and laid out very, ah, neatly, like a display, with each color selected to offset the others. Well, I didn't mean that it really felt lonely, but it's just that it's all alone, the water is all out here, like the ocean and the island is like cut in half by this gorge, it's really deep down, almost like you can't see bottom it's so dark so it's really almost like two but they're connected in there, and by this peninsula up here. Well, I don't remember what it was a fossil of, but it was a fossil, and it looks like this, sort of like a pre-historic animal with a big tail like this and because it was in stone it looked all rough like this but when it hardened and became a fossil it sorta cracked in the middle and the middle part was lost or something, see, here it looks like it's a V there, like it goes down in, it is all dark there and up here (*points*) where it's darker is kinda like a roughness that fossils have. Well, I don't see anything else in this one.

Well, I don't think it really looks like one, but when I first saw it I did, it's got these big stingers and it's all fat like they are and I think they might be orange and green like this is, the pink doesn't count. Well, I guess it could be like a face, not a real face but like a mask of a face, like an animal mask. Well, I think a beetle, they're black like this, like with a hard shell like this one has, and the little claws. Well, I think it's wider than this, but both halves are there, one on each side, it's the chestbone, I really am not sure if it's called the sternum but I think so, anyhow it's a major bone part, it just looks formed like a bone. Well, I think this might be two women doing something. Well, I thought of a trapper because it looks like he's in a fur coat of some sort which conceals some of his outline, especially his arms. Well, if I look at it this way, this part (*points*) could be a donkey I think; is that enough? Well, if I turn it over like this it could be some kind of design like they have on graves, like when they lay out the flowers. Well, if it were the same party these might be two other people, maybe men because they are thinner than the other two, as if they are dressed formally, see the heads and legs and these red parts would be the decorations for the party. Well, if it's OK. Well, if you know anything about dogs you know they play like this sometimes, sort of pushing their paws together, see they have their heads back and here is their ears, like they squat down a little when they do this, not this red stuff though, that doesn't count. Well, if you really use your imagination you could make it a mushroom too, the same shadowing effects would be for the basic shape of it. Well, if you've ever seen a caterpillar you know they look like this, it's just a side view of one in the profile you know, it really looks a lot like one. Well, I'm not exactly sure what it is, but it reminds me of the kinds of creatures from outer space, just great big things, see this one has big feet and little arms and it just looks like it's standing there. Well, it ain't dark enough to be fresh blood, it's lighter like dried blood, just a stain, and you can see the differences in the color like maybe it was still drying. Well, it could be a lobster. Well, it could be two ladies like at a picnic making something in this kettle. Well, it could have horns like a deer and these are the legs and it looks stretched out like it was jumping like they do a lot. Well, it does have these wings and the small body and it's all black or gray, whatever you want to call it, so it could be a moth. Well, it does look like a butterfly, I like butterflies so much, this one has pretty white marks so it must be poisonous. Well, it does look like a dog, see the legs and the head and body and these would be like rocks or something, the way they are colored it could be that he's in the forest or something. Well, it does sort of look like that, if you've ever made up a kid for a school play, like to be a clown, or for Halloween, that's how you might paint the lips, bright red and sort of in this shape, you just exaggerate the features, it could look like this. Well, it doesn't look like nothing. Well, it doesn't really look like real people but statues that are supposed to look like people, not this part but this (*points*), maybe like two women, I'm not sure, just like somebody made them to look like two people looking at each other, see the ponytails (*points*) and the nose and the chin, just like a side view. Well, it has a big ear like a donkey, and it's like he's just standing there, see (*points*), these are his legs and the head and this might be a tail; it really could be one I think. Well, it has a very irregular shape to it and the coloring is very much like furriness. Well, it has all the shades there, like to represent the disease, I don't know the name but the tree looks sick and the bark falls off, see, all the spots are like that. Well, it has that look to it, see these things go here and it's green in here like for the trees and such, each of those colors is for some kind of forest thing. Well, it has that shape to it and it's dark like an x-ray is, see, these are the upper leg parts and this is the pelvis (*points*). Well, it has that shape to it, sort of an hourglass shape like a keyhole, that's how they are. Well, it has the big wings, butterflies have those, and it has a little body like a butterfly, it just looks like one but not these parts out here. Well, it has the large wings like butterflies have and this might be the tail and the feelers in the front. Well, it has the pinkish-orange color just like when the sun hits water that's very still. Well, it has the shape like a cat and a small head, and the legs, and it just looks like a cat to me, one here and one here. Well, it has the shape of one and it's red like they wore years ago, I don't mean red masks, but very colorful ones. Well, it has the wings, look here (*points*) and these are the tentacles and this is the tail. Well, it has this whole body here and the face is like a bird and the big feet, just like some kind of monster, it's big-looking. Well, it has two animals on it, one on each side and a lot of different colors, it reminds me of something that might be on an environmental poster or button, this might be a tree on top I suppose if you use the middle too, it's just an emblem sort of thing. Well, it has wings and it's dark too, that's how moths are, not very pretty, just dull and dark, see, these are the antennae, it's not exactly like the other one, but it might be. Well, it just has that form to it, like a big bird, like a condor maybe or an eagle or some bird that has great big wings like this. Well, it just has that rounded shape to it like a flower, I'm not sure what kind, I believe that African violets are formed like this. Well, it just looks like one, a pelvis to me, that's all, it has that form to it, that's all. Well, it just looks like paint like somebody got mad and threw it and that's the way it landed, splat, just like that. Well, it just looks like the head of a person to me you can see the nose (*points*) and the chin and the forehead, just like a side view but I don't know anything else about it. Well, it just reminds me of mountains I think, the line is all jagged, you know? Well, it looks full, like the pinker area makes it look round at the sides, it has the effect of fullness and here is the top and the different colors make it look like it could be cut glass, you see the darker colors and the lighter colors give it a cut-glass look, like a very expensive candy jar or something. Well, it looks like a big bird that maybe somebody shot or ran over 'cause it's all blood and it's like dead. Well, it looks like that, see, here (*points*) would be the waterfall and this green stuff would be trees and bushes like in the forest, but the waterfall is way back in. Well, it really could be one, not exactly like the other one but a crab though; we go out to the beach a lot on the weekends or when I have days off and you see things like this, the round shells. Well, it reminds me of a gas-well explosion or something like that with the flames shooting out, see here. Well, it sure looks like one, they have a kinda wing part to them so that when they swim they really move fast. Well, it's all colorful like an eruption would be with the orange fire shooting outward and the pink would be some of the lava. Well, it's all different-colored lights like on a Christmas tree and here is the top where you put the star, and here are the two dogs too. Well, it's all furry, like the other one, you know? Well, it's all furry-looking the way the colors are there and it's sort of jagged around the edges like a pelt would be. Well, it's all in different colors, like they use to illustrate the different organs, like the liver and the stomach and the lungs, and maybe the chest bones here (*points*). Well, it's all red and see the pointed shapes, like an explosion. Well, it's an unusual-looking thing, something from the movies or something, all covered with fur. Well, it's been all torn up, like by a kid that caught it and now it's decaying, you can see the holes in it and it's all black like it was decaying. Well, it's big like a horsefly and it's got those white marks on it like they do, see the wings and these are the marks and the little feelers. Well, it's bigger like closer, it's all runny, see the lines in it make it look all runny like a pool of blood. Well, it's got big ears and skinny little legs like it was standing up like sniffing something. Well, it's got prongs on it and it just has that shape to it like one you use fishing. Well, it's got the wings out here (*points*) and the body part is smaller and here are the hands and the feet; do you see it now like I see it? Well, it's got these big legs, see here, and a small head up at the top part and well, it just looks like a skin, see the lines like on a bearskin (*runs finger over card*). Well, it's grainy-looking, the little markings in the color makes it look more grainy, not as pure as ice cream, more crystals. Well, it's in there, see the darker part is the snake and all this is a bush and it's like crawling through it, under it. Well, it's just alone, see the wings and the little body, it's kinda pretty, I'd like to see a real one like that. Well, it's just kinda like fog or smoke, there isn't much shape to it, but it's just all dark like fog or smoke, yeah, probably smog. Well, it's just like a bunch of colors bursting out all over, like a design that is created after the explosion. Well, it's just pink and long like bubble gum after you chew it, we used to do that all the time when I was a kid. Well, it's like a cat's face if you ask me, with a pink nose, not the nose, that's white, but the holes, you know, the nostrils. Well, it's like somebody took an axe and split this old rabbit right down the middle and it's sorta laid out there, see the leg here and one here. Well, it's like the face of a cat, it has the ears out here and the puffy cheeks, see here (*points*) and these are the eyes, kinda slanty like a cat and the mouth is here. Well, it's not a new one, it's like one of my grandmothers had, I think, a fur blanket, she said they used them in the car, see the fur is all there but part of it is gone, see the lighter places? Well, it's not a real flower, or at least I don't know what kind, but these could be the petals and it's like still not opened up all the way, all the different colored petals are there, like it may be opening now (*gestures with hands*) this would be the stem and the rest has just started to open. Well, it's not really here, I mean it doesn't look like light or light rays but the area sort of reminded me of that general image. Well, it's pink rather than the deep red of fresh blood and you can see the way the different colors are there that it's more like a dried stain, they're not uniform, so it looks dried up, OK? Well, it's pretty with the orange blooms or petals and the green is the leaves and this pink is the base, the root system. Well, it's shaped really well like a hair ribbon. Well, it's some kind of animal with its paws together one on each side, it has a small ear and the nose and the paw, see they are touching, one on each side, you can hardly make it out. Well, it's the same on both sides and you sort of get the picture of two animals on the sides, like gargoyles, I think they're sort of like lions but not really, see the legs and body but they have wings or something, like animals from mythology, it's all like a crest or emblem. Well, it's very colorful, with each color used to portray one part, like the pink might be lungs or something and so on, just an illustration, not the real thing. Well, its wings. Well, I've done pretty well on this. Well, just this part here, it's colored like an x-ray, black, you know, it's probably somebody. Well, let's see, this part could be the body part and this could be the wings out here. Well, like a group of them the way they are laid out there, it's really one cloud but it's sort of broken apart, like they were moving to take different positions. Well, like an irrigation ditch, it's dug down in, you can tell because it's darker than this other part, it looks muddy around it too. Well, one is up here and one down here but they are alike, just dogs, see the legs and the tail, I wish I had a dog. Well, part of it could be a fountain, this way maybe, with built-in lights, white lights. Well, part of it looks like two animals who are trying to get up this tree but I don't know what this bottom part is. Well, right now the pieces are laid out in a design like all the colors and the white parts still have to be filled in with other pieces of glass, when you make a stained glass window you try to use all different shapes for a special abstract effect, and this is how you might lay it out when you are beginning. Well see here, there's one here and one here and they're behind this big bush and they're waiting to eat something up. Well, she's not flying here, but it's like she has her wings out, like she is gettin' ready to fly, see the wings and she has little points on her cap up here and it's like she's standing on her tiptoes and see this top here is her cap, the points are probably magic too. Well, the head is right here (*points*) and the legs, front legs and they are yellow like collies are colored yellow like this. Well, the heads are back and here is the leg down here like you can't see the other one and each one has one arm out, just like standing there ready to begin doing something but not doing it yet. Well, the lights are on but it's not like a real house, more like a spook house. Well, the pink parts look like a couple of big flowers with the stems here and the rest is all made up with smaller flowers and foliage, I'm not very good about what kind of flowers but they are arranged well. Well, the red stuff is blood here and this looks like a piece of wounded flesh right here with the hole in it and the blood is coming out the front. Well, there are apparently two men here, dressed in formal attire, talking. Well, there are the holes in it too, but I think because it's all dark is mainly why I thought of decay. Well, there's not much fur left on it, just here in the center and the outer parts are all smudged like with mud or dirt. Well, there's sea coral there, it's the kind you can get bad cuts on. Well, these are her legs and this would be her shoulders and here are her hips and all, that's it. Well, these are wings and the head would be here and this black part would be the tail. Well, these little things are the claws and this center looks like the shellfish's body, and this is the tail but lobsters don't have a tail. Well, these look alive but they're not like real people, but they have little heads and sort of shapeless bodies, like gnomes, and they seem to be yelling at each other as if they don't agree on something, see, here is the face and the peaked heads and the rest is the body. Well, these side parts could be the two parts of the roots or something and they're coming together here and like pushing on the stalk here, pushing it upward and then it will get buds on it, it's not all there right now, it has to grow a lot before it gets the buds. Well, these would be the wings and the small body, it looks very much like a moth would look. Well, they are here and here, see, the long hair so they must be girls, little ones, and it looks like they're fighting maybe 'cause they're pointing in different ways, maybe they don't know which way to go and they're fighting about it with each other. Well, they are shaped like sun rays and they are behind this tree or post like the sun was just coming up. Well, they are small, like grasshoppers, and they have little antennae on them, and they're green too like a grasshopper, see one here and here (*points*). Well, they come out like this where the pointy part is and up here is where they get tied onto the line; my daddy takes me fishing sometimes. Well, they could be wolves I think, see the legs and they have that kind of body and the head kinda crouched in like a wolf and this thing in the middle could be a tree, see, it's pointed up here and these could be branches and this would be the ground I guess except some of the colors are all wrong. Well, they don't look like children. Well, they don't really look like people, but you could guess that if you let this top be the heads and here would be the hands and there are the bodies, the dark part. Well, they have all those legs like spiders but I never saw a blue one. Well, they have these small legs, there's one on each side, see (*points*) and they have these little antennae, like points on their heads. Well, they look like crabs with the long feelers, claws, and they got this weed or whatever between them and they're like fighting over it. Well, they look like they're pulling in different directions on this thing like they was each trying to get it for themselves, I can't see what it is but they are sure pulling on it. Well, they look like two cats, see the legs and head and tail and this center is like a tree, see the green on the top, it's kinda colored like trees in the fall and they're climbing it. Well, they look like two cocks to me, they have the peaks and the fat bodies and they're all red, like they get after a while, like all bloody. Well, they look very much like them and they're green, I think seahorses are usually green like this. Well, they make them like this, usually they put little wings on 'em like this, you can see a little figure of the body there and the wings like a voodoo. Well, they're all dark like storm clouds or something, just a bunch of them. Well, they're like lined up, see the two on the outside and two more in the middle but you can't see the two in the middle too well 'cause they are back in there. Well, they're like trying to pick something up or something you know, see this thing down here and here they are, see the heads and they've got their arms out down like here trying to get this thing. Well, they're not like real eyes, I mean like round, but they're like funny eyes like something from science fiction would have, maybe even two things, two eyes, one here and one here. Well, they're out here (*points*) and you can see this is a tree 'cause it's got a top and a middle and a bottom and they must have got stuck on it 'cause that's how they are. Well, this here is the ground and the hole, if it's a well it's just been dug 'cause there ain't no lining yet. Well, this here is the head and these would be the legs and this is their front part, that's how you can tell they're ladies 'cause they are bigger in front. Well, this is another you have to see in perspective, the white part here is the seat and this is the back and these would be the legs, sort of a low-back chair, like a special sort of Victorian chair. Well, this is like a different picture of the same thing, see this center would be like the backbone or something and there's a lung on each side, see they go upward like lungs are shaped and they have these little ends and they're all dark like it was the disease like they advertise, it's like the same lungs as in the other picture but taken from close-up and that makes 'em bigger. Well, this is the bear and here he's reflected down below and the blue is the water, water is blue like that and the rest is stones and things, all showing again in the water down here. Well, this is the head and here is the body, see the nose is up like he was honking for food the way they do in the circus. Well, this is the stem, like for the tree, and the dye markings on it create sort of a curled effect, like when leaves die they curl up like this. Well, this is the trunk part and the rest is just the head, see the way it's formed there? Well, this looks like a bag, you know, purse, and this looks like faces and breasts and limbs of women, see right here? Well, this looks like two people pulling something apart, they sort of look like cannibals. Well, this part (*points*) would be the waterfall part and it's kinda blue around it, like maybe the light was hitting it to give that blue color, it's light blue, but it's blue I'm sure. Well, this part down here is the part you put in the cork and this top part is what you turn, the handle, so as to get the cork to come out. Well, this top part would be the plant, see the branches here and this would be the pot down here, see, these would be the handles on it, it's almost like a small tree, or some kind of bush. Well, this way it looks like a piece of marble, we saw one once on a film about fossils and it sort of looked like this with the rough top part and some bigger cuts in it, like this middle part here. Well, thought it was a rocket 'cause it had fire. Well, usually they don't stick their heads out this far. Well, when I told my mom I was gonna take the inkblot test she said it had some bats, so this must be the one, see it could be two wings here and here and it really just looks like that; are we done now? Well yeah, it's got that fork part to it, we use them all the time where I work, you know, a crowbar. Well yes, to think of that emblem or copyright or whatever it is, the radiating light is an important part. Well, you can almost see it now, see the different colors, light here, that's the silver and darker here, that's the gold, like angels are. Well, you can see the forehead and the beard would be down here (*points*) and this would be the nose and chin, it just looks like that to me. Well, you can see the legs here and I guess this would be hands or something and I don't know what those bumps are, maybe knockers but that's kinda funny. Well, you can see the showy part, the darkness all around it and the white part is like the design on it, sort of like an abstract Indian design. Well, you can't see the foot well so it must be kind of curled up. Well, you can't see the head, except maybe just a little in the center and this is the leg and the rest is the big shell that they have. Well, you know they look all out of shape, like they are thin and they don't have much hair showing. Well, you know this is a tough one but I could make this top part into a cockfight, and they've really been at it 'cause they're all bloody. Well, you really have to use your imagination to see the tree, it's just this top and middle I guess but not the bottom, maybe it's like a couple of cats or something but they're not really pink, but the tree could be. Well, you use the same part as the vase but you put a tail on it, it would go down here, see this upper part would be the big round part and the tail would be down here, if I was going to draw a mushroom, that's how I'd make it, kinda using the shadowy effect to create the outline, making it darker like this is. Well, you're not crazy maybe, but they are real, I know, I don't want to look. Well-protected harbor but it's entirely too symmetrical for a harbor, peculiar contour; must be a coral island, not volcanic. What a happy picture. What a lot of colors, pink and yellow and blue and green. What made me think of it first was the butterfly wings there I guess and the body part in the middle. When butterflies glide they extend the wings forward like this. When I drink, I get hallucinations of rats going around in a circle, with me in the middle. When I first looked at it, it looked like a cat's head. When I look in the mirror – I don't see anything. When I was a kid, sissies always wore bow ties. When I was deciding on whether they were different I could easily have been confused. When I was younger my father used to spank me. When I was younger, my mother used an anal thermometer to take my temperature. When it hits it gives up a cloud of foam, and sunshine might give it the reddish color, background here seems way in the distance. When it splatters. When the bomb hits, it spreads out and this right here looks like the mushroom cloud and this up here looks like smoke and stuff. When you look this way it looks like a mad horse. Which means maybe it's a moth, but moths' wings are not shaped like that. White cotton ball. White dead bare branches. White house. White lines divide two lanes; in perspective. White thing started out distinctly, leaves fallen on whole pattern. White wings, circles being camouflage. Whole central area – no, maybe just this. Whole picture, some kind of philosophic aspirations of animal kingdom. Whole thing looks like an aviator, sitting on a stool, maybe awaiting orders. Why do I always get the shit end of the stick? Why would anyone want to do that to a dog? Wide sleeves, characteristic of a monk, or a professor, that kind of sleeve, but because of head or lack of hands I think it's less of a priest or monk, more of some supernatural creature. Wings are being spread out from the bottom. Wings, body, antennae. Wings, ears, tail-like structure. Wings go out like it's flying. Wings here, head could be here or here. Wings out flying. Wings outstretched, ears, can't tell which side is facing, a diagrammatic representation. Wire-haired fox terrier, the head is here, the shape and little furry around nose. Wishbone. Wishbone. Wishes never came true, but it was fun to pretend. Wishing I really had a mother, I don't, I never did. Witchy hats. With a large beard, large eyes. With horses' hooves for legs. With large ears; they seem sort of scared of each other; seem to want to run away and turning away. Without the support couldn't. Without them, they're helpless little creatures. Wolves looking off in different directions. Woman lying down with arms crossed. Woman's body doing a swan dive, with a man's head. Woman's figure without a head. Woman's shoe, heel. Wombs are shaped like this, like the hourglass of time and you can see this one is exactly like that. Women might wear such turbans but it made me think more of Turks because of the fancy clothing, heavy draped clothing. Would like to touch it, it's soft and maybe spongy. Yeah. Yeah. Yeah, a crab. Yeah, all over like somebody threw a lot of paint there. Yeah, all wet like mud, see these colors here (*points*) they're like mud. Yeah, bang, like a bomb is going off right there and you see the red fire shooting out like when bombs go off. Yeah, because it has those bulging eyes. Yeah, butterfly, well this is the wings and the body, see the wings are out like. Yeah, 'cause they're arguing – who is going to eat the children – 'cause I've heard a story about this witch. Yeah, from upside down it looks like a flower. Yeah, hair sticking up all over. Yeah, he's a big one too, boy he could really get you. Yeah, I guess so. Yeah, it just looks like a rain cloud. Yeah, it like folds inward, see here at the center, it looks like it goes inward like they do. Yeah, it looks exactly like a stingray. Yeah, it looks good like that like it's going up and down, except it would look more like one if it had some colors to it, this gray is dingy, see the rabbits on each end and the center would be the teeter. Yeah, it's big, massive, a gray hulk, looks like dirty snow all piled up like a snowman. Yeah, just all the inside parts. Yeah, just sort of a round green mess like you could almost grow penicillin in there. Yeah, kind of like looking at top view; see the line going down center? Yeah, like in pictures this center is the reactor and all the colors outside look like an explosion, a fission explosion or something like that, all colors, yeah, really like that. Yeah, like it's all red like rotted stuff gets red like this. Yeah, more like a bat. Yeah, one is sitting with his legs over the other's shoulders. Yeah, pretty much looks like something like a demon. Yeah, right in there (*points*). Yeah, see here, the outline could be steam. Yeah, see the wings here and the head and the feet. Yeah, standing together. Yeah, that's the one in the other picture too, it has these wings on here and here's those things like butterflies have on their heads, whaddaucallems they're right here. Yeah, that's what it looks like, right down in here, see, just this little part, like maybe the brain of a cat or rat or something small, and it's almost apart like those split brains are sometimes, see, a part is here (*points*) and the other part is here. Yeah, the black under the red, not the red but black, like the black tail of a raven. Yeah, the two pink creatures on the side look like moles. Yeah, these are the legs and that looks like the heads of beavers and these are their tails and this green looks like a trunk and they're climbing a tree, can I change it to a possum? Yeah, these are the women and this is the purse. Yeah, they have these big stomachs so the kids can punch 'em and these are clown ones but they make 'em in all different forms like seals and cats and things. Yeah, they just look like hands, see one here and one here, that's all, just hands. Yeah, this is the same color as rain clouds, it's dark gray, and it's the exact shape of rain clouds and this is the collision point down here. Yeah, this is the thorax, this is the head and these are the wings and it's grayish like moths I've seen. Yeah, this would be the eyes and the basic shape of the face. Yeah, two old ladies in two wheelchairs falling. Yeah, two people, this is the toe, hell, wide-trousered pants. Yeah, well they got blood all over themselves, maybe they aren't hurt but the blood might be from whatever they're fighting over like sort of animal that they killed. Yeah, wings are pointed downward, more like a bat in flight, not two-lobed like a butterfly. Yeah, with all the legs and the center is the shell part. Yeah, with the big ears out like a fox or something, see the white parts here are kinda slanted like foxes have and this is the nose and the mouth down here. Yeah, you don't use solid colors, but ones that have different shades or tones of colors like some of these here, you can see the different tones in them, deeper in some places and lighter in others. Yeah, you know they have this long thing coming out, I don't know if it's tails or what and they're round like this is here. Yellow spots, green, give the impression of a strung-out cat with moustache, green moustache, red eyes, yellow mark around them. Yep, it looks like one to me, see the face of it, here are the ears and it's got its tongue out like it was dead and there aren't no eyes, just holes like after you die. Yep, they're right there, and they're gonna kiss (*giggles*) so they must be in love. Yes. Yes. Yes, all of it again, these white parts would be the eyes and mouth I suppose. Yes, all of it looks like an abstract of some sort. Yes, as if the artist was trying to capture the intense force with all the colors and the lines emphasizing the moving upward of the explosion. Yes, his sense of humor, ability to care about others sometimes, his idealism, mixed with cynicism. Yes, I like it, it has beautiful wings and a larger than usual body but it's very poisonous, you can tell because of the white marks, look but don't touch you know. Yes, it all looks like one of those displays like you shoot up and it explodes into a pretty design as it falls, it just did that. Yes, it reminds me of the rabbit in *Bambi*, my son has me reading that to him all the time. Yes, I've always wanted to visit there. Yes, like collie dogs, see here is the head and the feet. Yes, right here (*points*) it's like a Scottie dog, just the head, like from the side, I know a girl that has one and it really looks like this, mostly because of the nose, it's flat like this. Yes, sort of like a dog, here is the snout and the head and this is a tail. Yes, that's right, it's the entire thing. Yes, that's right, these would be the wings (*points*) but not with the extensions, see this is the body and the antennae. Yes, this is the penis and this is the foreskin being cut off, it has the color of the foreskin. Yes, well it's very colorful with the animals on each side and I suppose each of the three mid-parts represents something of the family history. Yes, well moths are dark like this, it probably couldn't be a butterfly 'cause they're not dark, they have lots of different colors. You can almost see whiskers coming out (*shows with fingers*). You can always run away so that it doesn't hit you in the eye. You can imagine the whiskers protruding across the rest of the paper. You can see the different colors of the design. You can see the folds in here. You can't really make out their faces very well, they have little legs and weird-shaped heads and they're trying to hurt each other with this big thing in the center, this stick-like thing. You can't see all of them, just their heads and long necks, maybe they are special ones 'cause I think they aren't suppose to be black, almost all swans are white that I've ever seen. You can't see the whole dog, just from the middle, see mostly their heads, this (*points*) is the nose and the little ear. You ever see the pastries that people make? You have to cut out the rest of the picture. You know, all of it could be a plant, it would be a very exotic one I think because the orange petals, that's a very unusual color for a plant. You know, I see a split brain in there too, yeah, that's what it is, boy there's some funny things in these, it must be a small animal's brain 'cause it's so small. You know, if I turn it this way and leave out the red again it could be a rabbit sliding across a pond covered with ice. You know, if I turn it this way it looks like a bony structure, maybe like a pelvic bone. You know, if I turn it this way this part looks like a head. You know, it could all look like a big implosion too, like everything going in all directions and all the fire shooting up. You know, it could be a mask of some sort too, sort of a Halloween mask. You know, it could be a sick tree too, like they get a disease and turn funny colors and the bark falls off. You know, it looks like a couple of guys working on something. You know, it's like those muscle builders too. You know, that looks like a big gorilla and it's funny 'cause he's got boots on, which they don't wear, but he's kinda moving along there, like looking for something, kind of a big hulky thing. You know, that looks like sort of a lonely island, kinda all alone out there in the water with all them mountains and peaks, and a deep cut in there, just sorta feeling all alone sitting there. You know, that reminds me of fried shrimp, that's probably a funny thing to see. You know, that top could be a bullet too, like it just went through this stuff and it's coming out the other side. You know, the center part could be a top, like it was balanced like when they're spinning. You know, the colors in this part look like it could be a rock formation in the Painted Desert. You know, there's another white butterfly in there, maybe a moth not a butterfly 'cause butterflies aren't white, that's moths. You know, this green stuff reminds me of cheese after it gets all moldy, we went away for the week once and shut off the fridge to save energy but we forgot about some cottage cheese and it looks like this when we got back. You know, this little part here looks like a town or little village way off in the distance, one on each side. You know, this little part right here (*points*) could be a golf tee, I've caddied for my dad a couple of times. You know, this red part here could be like one of those hard-shell crabs you see on the beach sometimes. You know, this stuff looks like ketchup down here. You know, this thing that they are after could be another crab, but I don't mean for it to be with them, I mean if you look at it a little different, you know what I mean? You know, this top part gives a feeling of force, like something growing upwards, like forcing upward, like these are two plants and they've come together and they are pushing up, I don't mean two plants, but like parts of a plant and they form together here and this is the stalk going up. You know, this way it could be an eagle or hawk 'cause it has big wings, yeah, it must be a hawk 'cause them wings is so big. You know, this way it looks like a badge too, maybe like a Campfire Girl wears, or someone with something to do with the outdoors. You know, this way it looks like a stone crab, they got 'em in Florida, they're really good to eat. You know, this way it looks like a top like we used to have for my son when he was little. You know, this way it reminds me of those puppets you see on the TV sometimes, I can't think of who does them but they sort of look like this, like two puppets with the heads kinda back as if they're sorta in a position to do something but they're not moving yet, just in place ready to start moving like in a dance or something. You know, this way it's like them black lungs again but a lot bigger here. You know, this way the darker area looks like an x-ray of the pelvic area, you can see the pelvis and some of the bony structure of the upper leg. You know, this way you can see the heads of elephants. You know what this is? You know, you could make part of this like a face of a man. You might be in the country and see this after a heavy snowfall. You might get attacked, they get stuck in your head, I mean your hair. You must not have taken biology, they are just like this. You never really get to know anyone, there's always a mysterious part of them. You really can't tell what kind, just an insect with the wings out like it's flying and the head is here (*points*), weird-looking. You see it doesn't look very human and yet it's not an animal, this is the big tail and the feet and the little arms, he's sitting like on his own tail, it must be science fiction. You see the veins, different muscles, veins are usually in red. You try to allow for everything, but something unexpected comes up, things don't go your way. Your eye kind of follows this line downward, if you're standing back here. You're up very tall looking down. You've seen the pictures. Yuck, a snake up there in the bush, crawling along there; I don't like snakes do you? Yuck, that's funny, it's got two witches up here but they're not real ones. Yuck, this a black widow spider. Yuck, what's this?

Sources

1942 *The Rorschach Technique; A Manual for a Projective Method of Personality Diagnosis*. Bruno Klopfer. Yonkers-on-Hudson, New York: World Book Company.

1954 *A Rorschach Workbook*. Lucille Hollander Blum, Helen H. Davidson, Nina D. Fieldsteel. New York: International Universities Press, Inc.

1960 *A Rorschach Reader*. Murray H. Sherman, ed. New York: International Universities Press, Inc.

1976 *Rorschach Content Interpretation*. Edward Aronow, Marvin Reznikoff. New York: Grune and Stratton.

1974, 1978 *The Rorschach: A Comprehensive System*. vol. 1, *Basic Foundations*; vol. 2, *Current Research and Advanced Interpretation*. John E. Exner, Jr. New York: John Wiley and Sons.

1989 *Rorschach's Test: Scoring and Interpretation*. Alvin G. Burstein, Sandra Loucks. New York: Hemisphere Publishing Corporation.

Orthography in *The Inkblot Record* is consistent with these texts.

Typeset in Frutiger.

Printed at the Coach House on bpNichol Lane in Toronto, Ontario, on Zephyr Antique Laid paper, which was manufactured, acid-free, in Saint-Jérôme, Quebec, from second-growth forests.

Edited and designed by Darren Wershler-Henry
Copy edited and proofread by Alana Wilcox

Coach House Books
80 bpNichol Lane
Toronto ON M5S 3J4
Canada

416 979 2217
800 367 6360

mail@chbooks.com
www.chbooks.com